This book is dedicated to my family.

Faith and Family.
The pillars of life.

The Kevorkian Oath
by Richard E. Brown

ISBN 978-1-63393-088-9

This is a work of fiction. All the characters in this book are fictitious,
and any resemblance to actual persons, living or dead, is purely coincidental.
The names, incidents, dialogue, and opinions expressed are products of the
author's imagination and are not to be construed as real.

Published by

◄ köehlerbooks™

210 60th Street
Virginia Beach, VA 23451
212-574-7939
www.koehlerbooks.com

Cover designed by Kellie Emery and inspired by Katie Vespa.

THE KEVORKIAN OATH

A NOVEL

RICHARD E. BROWN

1

HOLDING ON TO A framed picture of his family, Eric Blumsfield was wheeled through a long, cold and caliginous tunnel. The walls were gray and unadorned: a windowless, colorless passage. Through his sedated eyes, the attendant pushing his wheelchair appeared to be wearing a long black hooded robe and carrying a long-handled sickle.

He was placed in a small room and left to himself. The room was cold and barren. There were no pictures on the wall and no soothing music. He glanced at the picture he held from last Christmas, where everyone was smiling and healthy. While hugging the frame he wondered if he would see them one last time. Would they walk through that door soon? How much time in this sterile hospital cell, alone?

Although he feared what was coming, he almost felt relief as the nurse entered the room to start his intravenous line. He thought she might at least say some kind and soothing words, but she was as silent as the barren walls as she placed the tourniquet on his upper arm and stuck him in the vein at his elbow—she didn't even smile. He almost cherished the feeling of pain as the needle entered the skin. Feeling pain was life, something he had never thought of before this moment.

The nurse taped it in place and started the intravenous fluid, which was frigid as it entered his body. He shivered as it coursed through his veins. He knew this was not a time to make the patient comfortable by heating the fluids. The nurse then left the room but not before removing the framed picture from Eric's free hand, and dropping it in the trash can. She exited without an utterance, seeming almost disdainful. Perhaps her lack of empathy was her only way of dealing with her job. Perhaps she was simply ambivalent.

As the fluid continued to flow into his arm, Eric thought of better times, youthful times, when life seemed as if it would go on forever. He had been so sure of himself and in what he believed. Now he sat alone, abandoned by his family and demoralized by his government.

※ ※ ※

Eric Blumsfield had been a prodigy, the brilliant son of two college professors. He started college at age fifteen and earned a medical degree before the age of twenty. He had firmly embraced socialized medicine, believing in a system where everyone had equal access to medical treatment. And, as a devotee to that principle, he publically advocated for a sweeping government program called the Medical Reconciliation Act, a new idea that, theoretically, would create a safety net of medical care, a system based loosely on European models.

"Money is no longer being wasted on extravagant treatments affordable to only a privileged few," Eric told a *New York Times* reporter. "We're placing emphasis on preventing illness, and curing treatable illness. We've democratized medical care."

Eric believed that preventative medicine for the young could avoid the long-term costs of extravagant medical or surgical treatment in old people. That meant having regular access to medical care for routine treatments and rewarding healthy lifestyles.

Eric took a position running preventative care clinics. He also volunteered abroad, enhancing his reputation. It was during one of these trips that he met his wife. She was a like-minded nurse who had accompanied his team on one of their trips abroad. Following their marriage, they had two young daughters, both healthy and beautiful.

Life was good. Work was good. Eric thought it couldn't get any better. He was right. A short time after taking over as a regional director of public health, he began having some mild, intermittent pain in his stomach. As is common for many medical professionals, he ignored it for several weeks thinking it would go away on its own. When the pain persisted, he tried taking antacids. He attempted to convince himself they were helping, but deep down he began to worry. His wife occasionally questioned him about it, but he brushed her off casually, telling her it was nothing.

He began to notice that his clothes were fitting a little looser, and a few people even commented that he looked like he was losing weight. Shortly thereafter, his skin began to turn a yellowish hue and the whites of his eyes were no longer white. He saw a doctor friend who ordered a magnetic resonance scan, which revealed a mass the size of a tennis ball in the head of the pancreas. Surprisingly, no obvious metastases were seen, so a surgical cure might have been possible, but his friends knew it made no difference. Eric's fate was sealed. The guidelines of the new Medical Reconciliation Act were clear on this diagnosis. *No treatment was successful often enough to warrant any expenditure for surgery or chemotherapy.*

Rumors of a medical underground had been around for several years, a place where sick people with some statistical chance of survival might be able to get treatment. But Eric didn't know whether such places existed. Even if they did, why would they want to treat him, one who had been such a strong and vocal advocate of the Medical Reconciliation Act? He knew such a selfish stunt would make it even harder on his wife and two daughters. The government would consider him a criminal, and his pension and life insurance would be forfeited.

With his wife's consent and encouragement, Eric decided he would perform his civic duty.

Doctor or not, he wasn't above the law.

❈ ❈ ❈

Eric sat sedated, alone in the cold room. The IV was having its intended effect.

The door again opened and a doctor entered. There were no comforting words. No one was holding his hand. The fluid felt even colder now as he watched the doctor take the cap off a needle attached to a syringe.

Eric's heart was pounding. He was more scared than he had ever been in his entire life. For the first time he wondered if there really was something after death. Would he see a bright light at the end of a tunnel or a loving God to welcome him to a new life? He only knew that he would find out soon.

Avoiding eye contact and without a single compassionate word, the doctor picked up the intravenous tubing and inserted the needle. Eric now thought his heart was going to pound out of his chest. He could hear every beat, and it rose to a thunderous roar. He wanted to scream, but he knew it would not matter. No one would hear him but this robot of a human in front of him.

As the doctor began injecting the fluid from the syringe into the intravenous line, Eric closed his eyes. He knew he would never open them again. His pounding heart quickly began beating erratically. He thought once again of his wife and daughters. Would they be okay without him? Would his daughters remember him? He truly hoped so. But what did it matter now? He would never know.

He felt no pain as his heart suddenly stopped.

2

"...AND ALTHOUGH IT'S HARD for us now to believe, it was not at all uncommon to spend over a half-million dollars to treat one individual with an incurable cancer. If only our government had been able to pass this act sooner, just think how much better off we all would be at this time in history."

"Can you believe we have to sit through this boring history class?" Samantha whispered. "I came to medical school to make life-and-death decisions, not listen to some old professor tell us what it was like in the Dark Ages of our grandparents. Look at this professor. I think it might just be time for him to be put out of his own misery."

"Oh, come on, Sam, don't you wonder what it was like before, when everybody was treated? Perhaps we were never supposed to play God."

"You can't be serious, JP."

"No, really. I think it might have been rewarding to give people some extra years on their lives. I know for myself, if my mother could have had a few more years with us when we were growing up, I would have liked it, even if she wasn't healthy all the time."

"Still, JP, just think of all the cost it would have taken to keep your mom alive for a little extra time. Your father may not even have been able to help pay for your medical school."

"Sometimes I'm not so sure I made the right decision anyway."

James Patrick was only in his second month of medical school, following a long tradition of doctors in the family. His grandfather had been a surgeon long before the Medical Reconciliation Act had gone into effect thirty years earlier. His father was caught in the transition and basically accepted his new role without argument. Although he had been personally opposed to the idea of doctors deciding who should live and die, he had felt it was inevitable that sooner or later the government would have to step in to control the growing cost of health care.

Once the Medical Reconciliation Act passed Congress and was signed into law, doctors were no longer guided by the traditional Hippocratic Oath. They were now given the power to withhold treatment based on probability tables. Initially, there was some opposition from both the public and the medical profession, but most soon decided it was for the greater good.

When prescribing medical treatment, doctors were required to use probability tables to estimate the chance that the treatment would be successful. Records were kept by the government on each doctor as to their ability to predict correctly. If a doctor's accuracy dropped below fifty percent, that doctor was required to take extra training on probability and statistics as well as refresher classes in his or her specialty. Doctors who continued to have difficulty predicting success rates after their remediation risked losing their medical licenses. A powerful federal institution called the Ministry of Health now policed the medical profession and its practices to insure compliance with what had simply come to be known as *the Act*.

As time passed, withholding treatment decreased overall medical costs, but not to the extent that had been predicted. Consequently, amendments were added to the Act which allowed doctors to not only withhold treatment, but also to decide which medical conditions were simply too expensive to treat. Individuals with lots of money and connections could seek treatment on the black market, often in other countries. Those less fortunate, whose families could not afford black market medical treatment, were terminated in End of Life Care Centers. Soon, however, the Civil Liberty Association sued the government over this inequality and pressured the politicians to end all care outside the Ministry's jurisdiction.

Shortly thereafter, the Ministry was given enforcement power to eradicate any black market facilities. Most facilities closed voluntarily for fear of the stringent penalties associated with ignoring the new laws. However, an underground of traditional health care providers persisted.

"...and we will continue from here tomorrow when class resumes," the professor said as the lights came on in the classroom.

"You know, JP, I wouldn't be saying things like that if I were you. You never know who might hear you and turn you in as a subversive. You are aware that the raids on the End of Life Centers have been increasing over the past year."

"Come on, Sam. I know things have been a little tense lately, but I still think we have freedom of speech. Don't you think you're getting a little paranoid?" JP said as he headed off to their next class.

"All I know is Dad seems more uptight these days and wonders why he ever took the job as regional director of the Ministry of Health."

Like JP, Samantha Atherton had come from a medical family. Her mother, father and two older brothers were all physicians. As an undergrad student, she had majored in music and dreamed of heading to Broadway, but she had felt obligated to follow the family tradition and become a doctor. Deep down, however, she knew it wasn't her true calling.

The University was spread out, and their next class required a long walk. JP, well over six feet tall, moved quickly, and Sam had to almost run to keep up with him. They had become instant friends after meeting on the first day of class and had been spending a lot of time studying together. Being around JP made Sam, at times, even forget her dreams of being a performer.

Halfway to their next class, a young man in a wheelchair approached them heading in the opposite direction. He had a backpack filled with his books attached to his chair. As the young man got within a few feet of JP and Sam, JP stepped off the sidewalk to make room for him to pass. However, Sam kept walking straight along the sidewalk. At the last minute, the young man rolled his wheelchair partially off the sidewalk almost turning over. Sam continued straight ahead as JP helped the young man right his chair.

JP jogged to catch up to Sam. "What was that all about, Sam?"

"What do you mean?"

"You almost caused that guy in the wheelchair to turn over. Couldn't you have moved and let him pass?"

"I guess so, but I just don't understand why they let disabled people on the campus. In fact, I'm surprised they even are allowed to exist, in view of the Act. After all, weren't you listening in our last lecture? The cost to take care of them must be astronomical."

"I don't know, Sam. That seems pretty harsh to me."

❋ ❋ ❋

As they arrived at their next building, the environment

changed dramatically. The well-lit classroom was circular, with sterile white walls giving it the appearance of a large hospital room. The students sat around the stage and the professor was in the center. Near the professor were two armed guards from the Ministry hovering over a patient who was sitting in a wheelchair, seemingly sedated. Her wrists were secured to the arms of the wheelchair by medical restraints. She was a pretty girl, probably in her early twenties. Her hair was long and dark and tied up in a ponytail. Although her clothes were institutional, they were clean and well kept.

Professor Samuelson started the discussion as the bell rang at the top of the hour. He was a short man with a rotund stomach. His hair was gray and thinned out. It was parted low on the left side and combed over in an attempt to cover the obvious bald area on top. A couple of students walked in late, drawing a scowl from the center of the stage.

In a raspy, gruff voice, the professor started. "I remind you that class will start promptly and end promptly. I'll keep my end of the bargain, if you all keep your end. Now, shall we begin?

"Miss Johnson is a twenty-four-year-old woman with very little past medical history. Until recently, she had been attending the university working on her master's in engineering. Her undergraduate degree was in mathematics, and she graduated with high honors. In fact, many of her professors were amazed at the quality of her papers. She has always lived alone during her education, and classmates noted that she had little to no social life outside the classroom. Miss Johnson was recently brought to our attention when she was seen in the restroom washing her hands over and over. She initially said she had spilled something on her hands and was having trouble getting it off. However, she was later seen in a similar situation. Now does anyone have any ideas regarding Miss Johnson's diagnosis?"

A few hands went up and the professor called on a young lady sitting across the room from JP and Sam.

"Could she have a problem with excess sweating in her palms? I think it's called *hyperhydradinosus.*"

"That would be hyperhidrosis. An interesting thought, but not correct. Someone else?"

Sam raised her hand. "Perhaps she has a phobia about dirt."

"Not bad for this early in your training. What was your undergraduate degree in?"

"Actually, sir, it was in music."

A few chuckles were heard throughout the large circular room. Again the professor flashed a scowl before he continued.

"Keep thinking. Your answer is only partially correct, but still very good."

JP noticed that Sam was beaming, but his main attention was on the patient. He couldn't understand what it must be like to be sitting in front of all these people like some lab specimen on display. He hoped she was indeed sedated.

Professor Samuelson continued. "Following these initial observations of Miss Johnson, further investigation revealed a similar pattern of behavior. The Ministry, therefore, felt obligated to have her examined. Her physician noted no anatomic or physiologic problem upon initial examination and referred her to Dr. Tomia in the psychiatry department. Upon further interrogation, she confessed to having obsessions about checking her door multiple times each night to make sure it was locked before going to bed, as well as many other rituals such as counting to certain numbers. Now can anyone further define the condition that Miss Atherton came close to diagnosing?"

A young man whom JP didn't know raised his hand. "I believe Miss Johnson exhibits the symptoms of obsessive compulsive disorder."

"Very good, Mr. Jones. That is the correct diagnosis. You'll be taught more in your clinical years about OCD, but I'll give you a brief overview to continue our discussion. It is thought that up to two percent of the population or even higher has some degree of OCD. That means that even a few of you may be hiding this disorder." The students in the class all furtively looked around the room. "Yes, I did say hiding it, because it is well known that many OCD patients are quite embarrassed by their problem and will be very secretive about it. In fact, prior to the Medical Reconciliation Act, OCD patients would frequently have symptoms up to ten to fifteen years before they were appropriately diagnosed and treated."

"Miss Johnson, would you be so kind as to tell us when you first noticed something was wrong?"

JP noticed the patient seemed almost startled at the professor's question. Once again, he felt sad for this young lady. She was quite pretty, and seemed to be Hispanic. He also saw a tear well in her brown oval eyes.

"Miss Johnson," the professor again broke the silence. "I repeat, could you please tell us a little bit about your condition?"

Miss Johnson sat motionless and tears began running freely down her cheeks. JP could almost see her trembling. He couldn't imagine what it must feel like sitting in front of all these people and be asked to spill your guts about an emotional problem. He could tell the professor seemed to be getting irritated with the patient, and deep down JP wanted to tell him to back off. But he knew that would be crossing the line.

Keep your mouth shut, he told himself.

"Well, it seems like Miss Johnson is not going to cooperate, so I'll fill you in on what has been gleaned from her interviews by our psychiatrists. Her first symptoms occurred when she was thirteen. Despite a lack of any precipitating event, she began feeling that she had do things in groups of four. If she didn't, she would feel severe anxiety and fear that something awful would happen to her parents. This ritual, along with others, has continued for the past eleven years and she was very good about hiding these symptoms from her mother and father. Her schoolwork did not deteriorate and, in fact, she excelled. However, she began avoiding social interactions as much as possible, and a few years later, she developed additional rituals such as turning light switches off repeatedly, or checking multiple times each night to make sure her home doors were locked. Again, as with many OCD patients, she was quite secretive about her rituals and was even able to keep it from her parents. It was not till she developed the repetitive hand-washing problem that her condition was identified. As it turns out, her parents had noticed something was wrong, but were afraid to confront her."

The professor continued as if Miss Johnson wasn't present. "I'm sure by now you're wondering what this case has to do in your beginning mathematics and probability course. We believe that there is no better way to introduce you to the importance and the power of statistical probability. Those of you who come from families in the medical field may realize how your parents' continued practice is, uh, shall we say, dependent on performance. There was a time when physicians worried tremendously about being sued by patients with bad outcomes. The Act ended that concern once and for all. That being said, physicians now have to live up to a higher standard than mere medical outcomes. They must provide efficient and cost-containing treatment for the greater good. This is where mathematics and probability take the spotlight.

"Now back to Miss Johnson. Can anyone tell me how successful the treatment of OCD has been in the past?"

JP knew the answer, but could not bring himself to raise his hand.

Sam, on the other hand, again seemed eager to make a good impression. "I'm not sure, but I do not think it is very successful."

"That's correct, Miss Atherton, but can you be more specific? After all, this is a mathematics and probability class."

Sam slowly sank down in her chair, and her face turned a little red as another student across the room held up his hand.

"Yes, Mr. Sampson?"

"From what I remember from my undergraduate psych classes, I believe most patients were helped by the treatment with medications that increased serotonin levels, with or without behavior modification, but the chance of a cure, per se, was negligible."

"That is correct, Mr. Sampson, there is no cure for OCD. In fact, it usually requires lifelong medical treatment and often behavioral therapy. It could be quite expensive. But I again remind you all that I'm looking for statistics and probabilities. May I remind you that Miss Johnson's outcome must be predicted before her fate is determined?"

JP cringed at the use of the word *fate*. The professor obviously already knew that there was going to be no treatment for Miss Johnson, and JP wondered if this innocent young woman also already knew her fate as well. He turned to Sam and whispered, "I can't believe this guy is talking like that in front of her."

Sam gave him a quizzical look as the professor continued.

"Well, I'm not going to belabor the point at this time. The main reason we are presenting these cases is to emphasize the importance of learning, not only the disease processes, but also the chances of cure and whether the patient can resume a good quality of life and, more importantly, a productive life."

The professor then motioned for his assistant to remove Miss Johnson from the classroom. JP could still see tears staining her cheeks as she was wheeled from the large classroom.

The assistant returned with a middle-aged man who was a little overweight and whose breathing seemed labored. The professor began giving the history of the man, but JP tuned out. He couldn't stop thinking about Miss Johnson. Several minutes later, Sam nudged him.

She whispered, "Earth to JP. You look like you're in another world."

"What? I guess I was thinking about that poor girl that just left. Did I miss anything?"

"Not really, just a little bit of the patient's history. He's basically forty-five years old and recently had a heart attack. Apparently his heart scan showed he lost about twenty-five percent of his heart muscle, and he also smokes."

"Thanks, Sam."

The professor droned on. "Now, due to the shortage of time remaining in the class, I'm going to show you how this math and probability class can help you in the future. You've just heard that his heart function has been diminished by his recent heart attack. Fortunately for him, it was a minor one. If, *and this is a big if,* he quits smoking and is able to lose fifteen pounds over the next month, the probability that he can still lead a productive life is sixty-three percent. On the other hand if he either resumes smoking or is unable to reduce his weight, the probability of recurrent problems within the next three years goes up to seventy-eight percent. That would put his cost-to-benefit ratio above the acceptable level. He has been informed of this and will be given thirty days in which to comply with his doctor's instructions. In addition, he will be blood-tested randomly for nicotine levels. I trust you all will study diligently as your future in medicine does depend on your ability to predict accurately. Next class we will start on your formal probability instruction. See you then."

Sam and JP got up and headed for the exit and the start of the weekend. "Are you doing anything fun this weekend?" Sam asked.

"My grandfather invited me over for dinner tomorrow night. You wanna come?"

"I'd love to, but my dad invited me to a Ministry dinner. I'll take a rain check."

3

CAPTAIN MIKE JAMESON SAT at his desk in the Ministry of Health. He had been head of the Medical Enforcement Unit (MEU) for the region for the past two years and was quite proud of the reputation he and his unit had built. They were respected as well as feared, a good combination as far as he was concerned. He had hoped to get a national position by now, but he would be patient. After all, he was only thirty-five years old and had started with nothing.

His father had abandoned him and his mother when he was just five. Mike barely even remembered him. His mother did the best she could, but having to work two jobs, she had little time to spend with him. Mike had loved his mom and enjoyed their time together. She had been energetic, upbeat and loving.

That had changed when she had developed breast cancer. Initial surgery had been successful, but the cancer had recurred less than a year later. For the next year he watched his mother suffer with pain and slowly deteriorate.

She had been released from the hospital and was supposed to

go to a hospice. However, she had refused and said she wanted to be with her son in her own home. Despite her sickness, she busied herself about their small house. She cooked and cleaned as if nothing were wrong, but Mike knew something was indeed wrong. She was thin and pale, nothing like she had been just a few months before. She had been vibrant and full of life. The cancer, something he really didn't understand, was apparently eating her from the inside.

Periodically she would stop what she was doing and would bend over holding her stomach, her face contorted, obviously holding back screams of pain. At times, tears would stream down her cheeks, yet she would look at Mike with a smile and say, "I'm fine. Go on out and play with your friends."

Mike rarely left her unless absolutely necessary. He felt helpless as she became weaker and weaker. The sight of her frightened him, but he forced himself to sit by her side. She was pale and gaunt and reminded him of a cartoon skeleton he had seen on television. In the end he was alone with her when she died. When she exhaled her last breath, he didn't cry. He felt she was better off.

※ ※ ※

After bouncing from relative to relative for ten years until he was eighteen, Mike had joined the Army, where he quickly surpassed his peers. He now felt like he was no longer helpless, in fact he felt superior. By the time his military stint ended, the Medical Reconciliation Act and the agency that would administer it were being ramped up. No longer would people have to suffer needlessly. Considering his Army training and disgust with traditional medicine, the Medical Enforcement Unit seemed like a natural fit for him. His rise through the ranks was unprecedented.

His big break came with the retirement of the predecessor of his present position.

With the success his team had had under his leadership, he was confident that a federal position in the MEU would be imminent.

Mike sat at his desk thinking about his mom when a knock on his door brought Mike to the present. His first lieutenant, Jaye Osgood, entered. He was tall and muscular, with a boyish look. He had been an excellent second-in-command, but was one of the few men in the unit that Jameson hadn't handpicked.

"Boss, we have news from an informant that a pharmacy across town is gonna be hit tonight by members of the Medical Underground. It seems like pretty solid information."

"Do you have a team gearing up for it?" asked the captain.

"Yes, sir. I have a couple of guys doing some reconnaissance. They're getting some photos of the area as well as a layout of the pharmacy."

"Good. Keep me informed. I may want to take part in this mission myself. Also, make sure we have adequate personnel at the End of Life Care Center. This could be a diversionary tactic, despite the reliability of your informant."

"Yes, sir," the lieutenant said as he exited the office.

Although most attacks had been on the End of Life Centers, attacks on pharmacies and pharmacy shipments had also been increasing. The Underground needed medicines to do their illegal care. He knew he had to devote men to this problem, but his personal focus was on the people in the Underground centers themselves. He couldn't understand how any medical doctor would want to prolong the lives of terminally ill patients or house those deemed unfit or unproductive, such as the mentally handicapped or physically deformed. The thought nauseated him, especially when he recalled that terrible year with his mother.

＊ ＊ ＊

Lieutenant Osgood returned with the mission plans that had been drawn up after his recon team returned. He planned to have men stationed in two of the surrounding buildings. The entry team would be in the armored vehicle parked in a garage one block away.

"That sounds good, Lieutenant. Is the pharmacy aware of what's happening?"

"The informant said the raid was supposed to occur after closing, sir, so we thought it wouldn't be necessary."

"Okay. But remember, I want to be there if at all possible. I'm supposed to attend the Ministry dinner tonight at the special request of Minister Atherton, so we'll have to wait and see when it all goes down."

"I'll let you know as soon as we get word," Osgood replied, turning to leave.

As the lieutenant left the room, the captain thought about the evening's plan. He really didn't want to go and socialize with the bigwigs of the Ministry, yet he knew he had to for his career. He would much rather be on the raid with his men. He would have to make sure the team at the End of Life Center was on its toes. He didn't want any mishaps occurring during the VIP Ministry of Health dinner. He would personally speak to the team on duty for the raid.

＊ ＊ ＊

Samantha really wasn't excited about the Ministry dinner, either, but her father wanted her there. This would be his first dinner since becoming the director, and she was sure he would want to show her off a little to his new friends. She didn't want to disappoint her father about that, or about her medical training, for that matter. Everyone expected her to be a star student.

She finished dressing just as her father and his driver pulled up to her apartment at six forty-five on the dot. She had finally chosen a long blue sleeveless gown with thin shoulder straps and a tight waistline. The gown showed just enough cleavage without being too risqué. Her father greeted her at the door.

"Sam, you look beautiful. Your mom would have been so proud of you. I hope the young men at the dinner will be able to keep their eyes off you."

"Come on, Dad. Please don't embarrass me tonight," Sam replied with a slight blush on her face.

The drive to the dinner was uneventful. She filled him in on her classes and told him about JP.

"He sounds like a nice young man. I'd like to meet him sometime soon."

"I'm sure you will, Dad."

※ ※ ※

Thomas and William were anxious. Although Thomas had been on many raids before, this one was different. Tom was a painter by trade and a good one. He had one living child. He had come from a large Catholic family and had hoped to have many children together with his wife, Jami. Their first child was a cute healthy little girl, now five years old. However, their second child had been born with severe Down's syndrome. After his birth, once his diagnosis was confirmed by the pediatrician, he was taken away to the End of Life Care Center. He and Jami had had almost no time to spend with him. Thomas had eventually adjusted, but Jami became severely depressed. She was treated for her depression for two months but failed to respond. She was taken from their home and Thomas assumed she too had joined their second child at the End of Life Care Center. It was then that he had made a commitment to the Underground.

At one point when he was young, he had thought about becoming a priest. However, the government had pretty much restricted what the church could do or say, so he had decided to fight his battles as a layperson. Life, in his opinion, was a gift from God and not something left to the whims of man. Fighting the establishment was, in his mind, as noble as serving the church. Both were about preserving human dignity.

William's anxiety was slightly eased by the fact that he was working with Thomas, who had transferred from an Underground faction on the West Coast. Thomas had been with the Underground for the last ten years and William took comfort in Thomas' extensive experience.

The men sat in an unmarked, nondescript van outside the hospital along with their driver, known to them only as Stanley. They were waiting for the call to proceed. Thomas was dressed as a doctor, complete with a valid ID card, and William wore an orderly's uniform. Neither man carried a weapon, since they would have to pass through a metal detector as they entered the hospital. Their target was a young lady destined for the End of Life Care Center. Their intel said she would be transferred that evening through the underground tunnel from the hospital. Their plan was to intercept the patient at the hospital. Once in the tunnel, it would be extremely difficult to escape except through the Care Center, which they knew would be heavily guarded by the Medical Enforcement team.

The call came. Thomas and William exited the van and headed toward the entrance of the hospital. Once inside the door, they passed without incident through the security checkpoint and the metal detector. Their target was supposed to be in her room on the fifth floor, so they moved directly to the elevators and headed up.

※ ※ ※

Across town, Lieutenant Osgood's team was in place. He sat with them in the armored vehicle, waiting for any signal from his lookout or any commotion from the pharmacy. His team had trained for various scenarios on a regular basis, and he had faith they would do a great job. Each team member was armed with an M4 assault rifle as well as a handgun. They were basically a specialized SWAT team.

Having been in position for almost an hour, he could tell that some were getting restless and wanted action. He hoped it would be an uneventful night for the team. He had been in the Medical Enforcement Unit for about ten years, but wasn't nearly as committed to its cause as his captain. He actually felt the Act was unethical. However, a job was a job, and he did have quite a large family to feed.

※ ※ ※

Samantha and her father, Dr. Atherton, arrived at the Ministry dinner just as most of the other guests were arriving. The dinner was being catered in the atrium of the main building. The atrium was ornately decorated for the event, featuring several ice sculptures and an astounding number of freshly-picked flower arrangements.

Many eyes were on Sam as she entered the atrium. In her blue evening gown, she strolled gracefully alongside her father. A string quartet was playing music and the atmosphere was quite lively. Dr. Atherton introduced her to everyone who approached, and she tried to be as engaging as possible. Fifteen minutes after they arrived, a ruggedly handsome man approached. He was tall with dark hair and, even with his suit coat, she could tell he was quite fit.

"Good evening, Dr. Atherton," the man said, extending his hand out to Sam's father.

"Good evening, Captain. I'm so glad you could make it. I take it everything is quiet on the security scene."

"So far, but the evening is young."

"Well, I'm sure you have everything under control. I've been reviewing your record since your arrival here. Pretty impressive, I must say."

"Ahem," Sam said as if clearing her throat.

"Oh, I'm sorry, dear. This is Captain Mike Jameson. He is in charge of our Medical Enforcement Unit. Mike, this is my daughter, Samantha. She just started medical school here a few months ago."

"Very nice to meet you, Samantha," Captain Jameson said extending his hand out to Sam.

"Please call me Sam," she said, now thinking that the evening might be more fun after all. Her father excused himself and Sam and Mike continued their conversation.

✳ ✳ ✳

The alarm in the pharmacy triggered just as Thomas and William reached the elevator in the hospital. Lieutenant Osgood quickly radioed his lookouts.

"Tony, you see anything on white?" Osgood referred to the front of the pharmacy.

"Nothing here, Lieutenant."

"Russell, anything on black?" This referred to the back entrance to the pharmacy.

"Nothing, Lieutenant."

"Okay, let's hit the pharmacy now!"

※ ※ ※

At the hospital, Thomas and William exited the elevator and made their way to Room 514. The nurse in the hallway briefly glanced their way and then returned to her computer, inputting her patient's data. They entered the target's room and saw an empty bed. After a brief moment of panic, Thomas cleared his head and exited the room heading for the nurses' station.

As he approached the station, a clerk looked up and said, "May I help you?"

Thomas replied, "Yes, I'm Dr. Stevens from the Ministry of Health. I am here to interview Ms. Johnson before she heads over to the End of Life Care Center. Do you know if she has been sedated yet, and by the way, why is she not in her room?"

"I'm sorry, sir. She was sedated about an hour ago, and the orderly just left a few minutes ago to take her over to the Care Center. You might be able to catch them before they reach the tunnel if you hurry."

Thomas quickly thanked the young lady and casually headed back toward the elevator where William rejoined him.

"They've already picked her up and headed for the morgue." *Morgue* was the name the Underground called the End of Life Care Center.

"What should we do, call it off?" William asked.

"No," Thomas said as he pushed the elevator button for the basement level. "Let's see if we can catch them before they reach the tunnel."

※ ※ ※

The entry team lined up along the door of the pharmacy waiting for the lieutenant to give the order. The pharmacy was located on the first floor of an old two-story brick building. The front entrance had an aluminum outer door and a thick inner wooden door with a deadbolt lock. The lead man approached the door while a second man moved out with him as protection.

They radioed to the lieutenant, "Ready at entry."

"On my command, one, two, go!"

As the lieutenant said "go," the lead man opened the outer screen door while the second man used the battering ram to break the deadbolt clean out of its mounting in the adjacent wall. The alarm continued to blare as the third man tossed in a flashbang. After the loud bang and flash, the team passed the lead man and entered the smoke-filled pharmacy. They split into small groups and methodically cleared each aisle of the outer pharmacy. They then moved back to the closed offices and entered them as they had the front door. "Clear" could be heard as each room was again methodically checked. No inside stairs to the second floor were located.

※ ※ ※

Thomas and William reached the lower level and headed toward the entrance to the tunnel. As they approached the door they saw a fully-armed MEU officer standing guard. They quickly ducked into another hallway before he could see them.

"Now what?" William asked Thomas.

It would be Thomas' decision whether to proceed or withdraw. After just a brief thought, he said. "I say we see if we can gain entrance to the tunnel. Perhaps we can intercept her before she reaches the morgue."

"I'm in. Let's see what the guard says. The most he can do is deny us entry. At least, I think that's all."

Thomas stepped back into the hall leading to the tunnel entrance and the guard while trying his best to look calm and composed despite the pounding heart in his chest.

＊ ＊ ＊

Sam finished her dessert as she continued her conversation with Captain Jameson. She found him quite alluring. Her father had left them alone at the table most of the evening while he made the rounds making sure everyone was welcomed and having a good time.

"So, Mike, do you get much time off?"

"Enough. But I still have to keep in touch with my team at all times."

"Well, perhaps we could get together for a drink or dinner sometime."

"I'd like that. You don't think your father would have a problem with that?"

"Well, you know, I am a big girl now."

Captain Jameson smiled, but before he could answer, his phone rang. She could tell he was not happy with what he was hearing on the other end. Lieutenant Osgood had just filled him in on the situation at the pharmacy.

"Do one final check around the building yourself, and also get the owner down there and grill him. Make sure he didn't have anything to do with this. Also, track down that informant and make sure he doesn't feed us any bad information in the future."

At that he disconnected the call and quickly placed a call to the End of Life Care Center.

"Sergeant Michaels, this is Jameson. Our team just came up dry at the raid so it looks like it could have been a diversion, although it could have been just some bad intel. No matter what, keep a close eye on things there and double the guards in the

Center for the next couple of hours."

"Yes, sir," the sergeant responded and hung up his phone.

Sam queried, "Trouble?"

"Probably not. Just trying to make sure."

※ ※ ※

Thomas and William approached the guard. William felt trepidation, but Thomas confidently addressed the guard and handed him his ID card.

"I'm Dr. Stevens from the Ministry. I was supposed to interview a..." He glanced down at his clipboard casually and then looked back up. "...Ms. Johnson before she was transferred to the Center. Unfortunately, we just missed her up in her room. Has she already gone by here?"

The officer looked somewhat skeptical but politely responded. "You just missed her. In fact, I'm sure she's probably still in the tunnel."

"Look, I really need to ask her some exit questions. If I don't I'm gonna catch hell from Director Atherton, my boss. Could we just go in and ask her a few in the tunnel and then let her go on?"

"I'm not supposed to let anyone but transportation and the patient through here."

"Come on, man, this would really save me a lot of hassle. No one will know."

Before he could answer, the guard's phone rang. "Yes, sir, everything's quiet over here." He again listened and then replied, "Yes sergeant, I'll be right over," and then hung up.

William's hopes were dashed, but the officer said, "Look, I've got to report over to the Center. You can walk with me through the tunnel. If we catch them, you can ask her a few questions. If not, there's nothing else I can do for you. You'll have to exit back through the hospital, otherwise my sergeant will have my ass. The orderly should have a key card to get you back through the tunnel door."

Thomas gave a quick glance at William who nodded affirmation and then he replied, "Thanks, officer. That sounds like a good plan to me. At least it gives us a chance of staying out of trouble."

At that, the officer opened the door with his key card and Thomas and William followed him quickly into the tunnel. The tunnel was cold and dim, in keeping with the mood of those being taken for their last journey. Nothing adorned the walls. Thomas felt a chill just thinking about all who had passed through this avenue of death. They caught up with the orderly and the patient near the end of the tunnel and Thomas caught the orderly's attention. The officer proceeded without stopping or saying anything to the orderly.

The orderly seemed somewhat confused as Thomas introduced himself as a doctor from the Ministry. He had never had anyone stop in the tunnel before, and he quickly became suspicious. As Thomas spoke, William moved around the wheelchair and pretended to look at the patient who seemed oblivious to the world. He cautiously slipped a flashlight out of his jacket and struck the orderly on the head. They carefully lowered him to the floor, took his key card, and grabbed the wheelchair, before quickly retreating back through the tunnel.

※ ※ ※

Inside the End of Life Care Center, security was tight and all officers were on high alert. The sergeant reported back to Captain Jameson by phone.

"Sir, we doubled the security in the center and all seems quiet at this time."

"That's good."

"Just a minute, sir."

A doctor exited the treatment room and approached the sergeant while he was still talking to the captain.

"We've been waiting for a transfer from the hospital. She is at least fifteen minutes overdue. Has anyone come through the tunnel?"

At that the sergeant stiffened and said to the captain, "Sir, I'll get back with you. I need to check out something." He hung up the phone and asked the doctor what floor the patient was coming from and quickly placed a call to the fifth-floor nursing station.

"Yes, this is Sergeant Michaels in the Care Center. We've been expecting a patient from 514 for some time now. Is she still on the floor?"

"No, sir. An orderly left with her probably twenty minutes ago. She should've arrived at least ten minutes ago. You know, there were two men here from the Ministry looking for her after she left. The doctor said he had some questions for her before she went to the Center. I think they headed to the tunnel to try and catch her there."

The sergeant hung up the phone, obviously agitated. He called for two other men and headed towards the tunnel. Just as they arrived, they heard pounding on the other side of the door. They quickly opened the door and found an orderly holding his head. The orderly described the two men to the sergeant.

✳ ✳ ✳

Thomas and William, along with the young woman in the wheelchair, exited the tunnel and headed for the elevator. Thomas knew they had just minutes before the orderly would be found or the patient would be missed at the morgue.

They took the elevator up to the lobby and headed toward the front exit. Just as they approached the door, a Medical Enforcement officer approached them and held his hand up motioning them to stop. Thomas held out his ID and said, "Good evening officer. We're just taking the patient out for a short walk."

The officer looked at them suspiciously and noted, "She looks awful sedated to be going out for a walk."

"We were here interviewing her and, unfortunately, they had already administered her evening medications. We thought a bit of fresh air might help her answer our questions and save us a trip back tomorrow. It shouldn't take long."

The officer again looked at each one of them and then motioned for them to pass.

William pushed the wheelchair through the door as Thomas held it open looking as casual as possible. They meandered down the ramp while looking around for their van. Stanley spotted them and starting pulling the van toward them.

The officer was carefully watching them through the window as his radio blared out a warning about two men dressed as a Minister of Health doctor and an orderly that were abducting a patient scheduled for the End of Life Care Center. He opened the door just as the two were loading the patient into an unmarked white van. He ordered them to stop, and receiving no response, he pulled up his rifle and fired several rounds as the van sped away. Bullets sprayed the passenger side as the van sped off.

※ ※ ※

The patient and William had slid into the back seat and Thomas in the front.

"Looks like we made it," Thomas said as he turned to check on the patient and William behind him.

The patient sat upright with a blank look on her face. She was rubbing her hands over and over as though she was trying to clean them. He then glanced over toward William, who was sitting in the seat, but his head was bent down. A large red spot was forming on the white orderly shirt. Thomas reached back and touched William's wrist, feeling for what he feared wouldn't be there—a pulse.

※ ※ ※

The evening was drawing to a close at the Ministry dinner, and Sam was disappointed that she would be leaving her new acquaintance.

"Do you have any plans for after the dinner?" Sam asked. "I would love to leave and get a drink."

Normally, Mike would have jumped on this invitation, and, then usually would wake up next to the lady the following morning, but he was hesitant. This was Sam Atherton, daughter of Dr. Atherton, his superior officer. A one-night stand wouldn't be a smart move for anyone in Mike's position, but serious dating wasn't a priority, either. Although, if things went well, being in a relationship with the daughter of the Director of the Ministry of Health couldn't hurt one's career.

"That sounds quite tempting, but, I don't want to upset the boss."

Sam smiled and said, "I told you, I'm a big girl now." He gently grabbed her arm and they headed over to where her father was saying a few goodbyes.

"Daddy, Captain Jameson and I are gonna go out for a drink. Do you mind if I pass on the ride home?"

Dr. Atherton gave a furtive glance at the captain and said, "Not at all. Just be in by midnight." At that she giggled, and just as she and the captain headed for the door, his phone rang.

"Captain, this is Sergeant Michaels. I'm afraid we had some trouble at the hospital." He informed Jameson about the abduction.

"Shit!" he said as he hung up his phone. "Excuse me, I'm sorry. I'm afraid I'm going to have to take a rain check on that drink. Duty calls."

"Nothing serious, I hope," Sam replied.

"No, just a little incident at the hospital I need to check out."

Sam gave him her phone number as he left and then headed back to her father to get a ride home.

4

JP WAS ON HIS way to his grandfather's house for dinner. He was happy classes were over for the week. Today's class, with the young lady on display like some lab animal, left him with a sick feeling in the pit of his stomach. He had hoped Samantha would join him for the evening to help take his mind off the young patient with OCD. He was also wrestling with what to do about Sam. He was developing romantic feelings for her, but couldn't tell whether she felt the same way.

Visiting his grandfather always seemed to make JP feel better. His grandfather was somewhat of a Renaissance man. Although his career had been in surgery, there wasn't much he hadn't done at some point in his life. JP had heard stories of great adventures from his grandfather over the years. At first, JP thought his grandfather had been making up most of them, but the more he got to know his grandfather, the more he began to believe they were all true.

While in college, his grandfather had obtained his pilot's license and lived up in Canada as a bush pilot, flying hunters up into northern Canada to remote areas for exotic hunting expeditions. He had many tales of daring landings in open fields and on small lakes as well as run-ins with numerous bears and wolves.

His brief bush pilot career had been followed by a three-year stint as a Navy corpsman. He had fought in Iraq and Afghanistan with a Marine recon unit. Numerous Marines owed their lives to his grandfather, as evidenced by the many Christmas cards he received each year. After being discharged, he had published a book of sketches he had drawn during the two wars. Many won high acclaim from the world of art, and many were on display in the Museum of Marine History.

His experience as a medic convinced him that medicine was where he belonged. He had subsequently enrolled in medical school, somewhat older and more experienced in worldly matters than most of his fellow classmates. This, along with his high intellect, allowed him to excel in medical school as well as in his surgical residency. He had practiced surgery for more than forty years, loving every minute of it. His most enjoyable times had been his annual trips to various underdeveloped countries, operating on those less fortunate than his patients back home.

JP's grandfather lived just on the outskirts of the city, but all in all, it was usually a fairly short drive for JP. However, tonight, with his mood in the gutter, it seemed to take forever. It was cold and raining, which added to his gloom. He finally arrived and pulled into the drive.

The house was a small one-level home with an attached garage. The yard was meticulously manicured by his grandfather, who had a surgeon's attention to detail. JP opened the outer door and gave a soft knock.

A gentle-appearing man who looked twenty years younger than his age of eighty opened the door. He was a bit shorter than JP but stood as erect as a young Marine at attention.

"Hi, JP. Come on in. It's good to see you again. I was hoping to see you more often since you're in school here, but I'm sure they're keeping you pretty busy."

"You know it, Grandpa," JP replied. "How's everything been going with you? You keeping busy and out of trouble these days?"

"Oh, you know how it is when you get old. Go to bed at eight and get up at five. Drink coffee and read the newspaper. Take a nap. Have lunch. Sit on the porch in a rocking chair. Take another nap. Have supper. Go to bed. Then start it all over the next day," he said with a slight chuckle.

"I know you better than that. You've probably been climbing mountains and chasing women."

"Very funny, young man. Women have been out of the picture since your grandmother died. Now, mountains, on the other hand..."

They both walked into the living room. His grandpa motioned for him to have a seat and then disappeared into the kitchen. JP looked around the room at the several framed ink and pen sketches on the wall. The detail of the sketches was remarkable, depicting scenes from the wars that made JP feel as though he was there in person. The furnishings of the room were fairly simple, which was not surprising, since his grandmother had believed in living a simple and unassuming lifestyle.

As he looked further around the room, he saw another framed picture he hadn't noticed before. He walked over to it to get a better look. Upon closer inspection, he saw that it was a sketch of a doctor in surgery. Superimposed on the sketch was what looked like a poem or a speech:

The Hippocratic Oath

I swear by Apollo, Asclepius, Hygieia, and Panacea,
and I take to witness all the gods, all the goddesses, to

keep according to my ability and my judgment, the following Oath:

To consider dear to me, as my parents, him who taught me this art; to live in common with him and, if necessary, to share my goods with him;

To look upon his children as my own brothers, to teach them this art.

I will prescribe regimens for the good of my patients according to my ability and my judgment and never do harm to anyone.

I will not give a lethal drug to anyone if I am asked, nor will I advise such a plan; and similarly, I will not give a woman a pessary to cause an abortion.

But I will preserve the purity of my life and my arts.

I will not cut for stone, even for patients in whom the disease is manifest; I will leave this operation to be performed by practitioners, specialists in this art.

In every house where I come I will enter only for the good of my patients, keeping myself far from all intentional ill-doing and all seduction and especially from the pleasures of love with women or with men, be they free or slaves.

All that may come to my knowledge in the exercise of my profession or in daily commerce with men, which ought not to be spread abroad, I will keep secret and will never reveal.

If I keep this oath faithfully, may I enjoy my life and practice my art, respected by all men and in all times; but if I swerve from it or violate it, may the reverse be my lot.

Just as JP finished reading the oath, his grandfather returned from the kitchen with some hors d'oeuvres, fresh from the oven.

"What do you think of that oath? Seems to be a far cry from where we are today doesn't it?"

"I've never heard of this before. There was sure no mention of it in our history class. Was Hippocratic a person?"

"You bet, JP, but he was actually Hippocrates. He used to be called the Father of Medicine. He lived several hundred years BC and actually taught students medicine or, I should say, what was the medicine of the time. In fact, I took a more modern version of this oath when I graduated from medical school. Most medical schools used to have all their graduates recite some version of the Hippocratic Oath. Unfortunately, this practice was dropped sometime before the Medical Reconciliation Act took effect. The idea of doing no harm became somewhat, shall I say, politically incorrect, as you might have guessed. Thank God I retired by that point."

"Why do you say that, Grandpa? Did you really treat everyone and everything? Surely there must have been times when you withheld treatment or decided not treat someone."

"Well, JP, of course there were times we decided not to treat someone. However, this was only done after a compassionate discussion with the patient and his or her family, not based on some actuarial tables, and definitely not based on threats from the government. Being able to talk to patients and discuss such options in a compassionate manner was part and parcel of being a good doctor."

"Well, how did things get like they are now so fast?"

"That's a long story that started a long time ago. It didn't just change overnight. It was a slow process partly by the design of some social elitists, or progressives as they like to be called, and also due to the apathy of a large part of the population. As far back as the beginning of the twentieth century, there were those that believed the government should control most aspects of the people's lives. They believed people were incapable of making educated and appropriate decisions for themselves. For a time they were kept in check. Then, during the first Great Depression in the 1930s, an entitlement philosophy took hold. At the time, with unemployment at twenty-five percent, it was necessary for the government to do what they could to help the people without work."

"That sounds pretty reasonable to me," JP interjected.

His grandfather motioned him toward the kitchen and, as they sat down, he continued. "Unfortunately, once the Depression ended, some of these programs persisted. This led to dependency on the government. Had the programs stopped then, perhaps things would have never gotten so bad, but they didn't stop. As the population aged, a program called Medicare was started to deal with the cost of health care for the elderly. Along with that, another program called Medicaid was started to provide care for poorer people unable to provide care for themselves or their dependent children. On the surface, these programs appeared to be good for society and, therefore, won approval. However, with the deterioration of the family unit starting in the sixties, the number of people on Medicaid grew exponentially, which began to bankrupt many states. This, coupled with the fact that both programs were run by enormous government bureaucracies, caused huge deficiencies in the delivery of health care."

"Why didn't people address these problems at that time?"

"That would have made sense but, unfortunately, the politicians didn't want to alienate their constituencies. Let's start eating, and we can continue this discussion later."

Cooking was just another one of his grandfather's many talents. The meal he prepared could easily have passed muster in a five-star restaurant. The dinner conversation was much lighter, and his grandfather regaled JP with many more adventures he

had not previously heard. Following dessert, his grandfather
again motioned for them to return to the living room.

"Now where were we with that history lesson?"

"You had just mentioned the Medicare and Medicaid programs."

"Oh, yeah. Well, I think if things had remained like that, medicine still wouldn't have gotten into the shape it's in now. At that
time, the cost of health care was still just about thirteen percent
of the gross national product. High, no doubt, but manageable.
Unfortunately, there were many people who fell through the
cracks, so to speak. They made too much money to qualify for
Medicaid, but felt they couldn't afford private health insurance. I
might add that there were many who also just elected not to buy
any health insurance. At any rate, around that same time many
liberal politicians were using this group of uninsured people as a
pawn to force some sort of nationalized health care. They would
point to other countries and boast of their universal health care
systems, while at the same time exaggerate the problems with
our own system. Their mantra became *Health Care is a Right!*
not a privilege, as many of us saw it. This was especially true for
those of us who had seen the health care in most Third World
countries. Many unions would go on strike just because their
companies wanted them to pay for their health care. Yet those
same people thought nothing of spending hundreds of dollars on
sporting events or other types of entertainment."

JP was amazed how none of this had even been mentioned in
history classes. They had been fed basically what the bureaucrats
wanted them to hear.

His grandfather continued. "Despite all this, there were many
good people who believed that the government would not be
able to run an effective health care system. They resisted long
and hard, but eventually the social elitists were able to convince

enough people that the government could do a better job. They slowly were able to get bills passed through Congress. They hid laws deep within bills that had nothing to do with health care, but which gave increasing control to the bureaucrats in Washington, D.C. Doctors and hospitals were monitored, and those who didn't conform to the new rules and regulations were fined heavily or totally relieved of their privileges. It was just a matter of time until they had complete control."

"That explains the universal health care system, but not the policies of restricting treatment or terminating patients. How did we possibly get to that from the way you treated patients?" JP questioned.

"Well, other things were going on during this time as well. In 1973, the Supreme Court legalized abortion in a case called Roe vs. Wade. Many people at that time thought that could be the beginning of a slippery slope, but despite the objections of many Christian organizations, people slowly became somewhat indifferent, and soon even very late-term abortions became fairly standard. It wasn't long before people began using such things as amniocentesis and sonograms to more or less decide *in utero* if the baby was worth keeping. Some bioethicists even went so far as to say a child really wasn't even a human being until he was a few years old."

"Is all that why I've never seen an adult with Down's syndrome?" JP queried.

"Yes, that, as well as the fact that the one of the first parts of the Act was to round up all mentally challenged individuals for termination."

"I still don't see how abortion and the government control of health care eventually led to the End of Life Care Centers."

JP's grandfather liked that JP was so interested in the politics of the current health care system. He was especially encouraged by the fact that JP seemed upset about the End of Life Care Centers. He continued with his history lesson.

"I am as surprised as you are that we got to this point. Despite abortion, I never thought doctors would be forced to make decisions about terminating people. In 1989, a so-called doctor who was actually a pathologist made headlines as *Dr. Death*. His real name was Jack Kevorkian. He assisted people in terminating themselves by providing them with an anesthetic agent. He technically didn't administer the agent, but for all practical purposes, he was terminating the people. He managed to get away with it for some time, but was eventually convicted and put away. It wasn't long after that that states began passing euthanasia laws, which allowed physicians to do assisted suicides."

"A friend of mine who's a senior at our school was talking about his graduation and mentioned something about a part of their ceremony where they take an oath similar to what you showed me earlier, but I think he called it the *Kevorkian Oath*."

"I'm not surprised at all by that. Just prior to the passage of the Medical Reconciliation Act, there were many bureaucrats hailing Jack Kevorkian as the new Father of Modern Medicine. Idiots with no medical training referring to that psycho as the *Father of Modern Medicine,* it made me sick to my stomach."

"He hardly sounds like a man of the stature of Hippocrates," JP said.

"You're absolutely correct. There is one final factor that really helped to bring about the current state of medicine. As you might have expected from what I said, the government was no better than the private sector in controlling the cost of medical care. The people still wanted the best of everything when it came to their health care since they had been duped into thinking that health care was an entitlement. Once the bureaucrats took over, they realized this, and that's when things began falling apart.

They knew that the only way to control the cost was to restrict the care. It was just a matter of time before they came up with the Medical Reconciliation Act. There were some objections at first, but most realized it was too late. Their complacency had doomed them much earlier."

"I can't believe Dad went along with all this."

"Your father really didn't, but with a family to raise and educate he believed he had no choice."

"Still," JP added, "I just can't see Dad sending someone to the termination center."

"I'm sure it hurts him deeply, but like most of the doctors, he really has no choice but to comply or quit."

"I'm not so sure I'll be able to make those kinds of decisions in the future."

As his grandfather started to reply, a cell phone rang. His grandfather excused himself and stepped out of the living room as he answered his cell phone. JP again glanced around the room and noticed another framed quotation. He stepped over and picked up the small frame from the end table:

A government big enough to give you everything you want is a government big enough to take away everything you have.

—*Gerald Ford*

His grandfather returned from the kitchen as he was setting down the frame.

"Pretty prophetic, don't you think?" he said.

"Yes. And terrifying."

"JP, something's come up, so I'm gonna have call it an early evening. I need to go check on a friend who's not feeling well."

"Would you like some company?" JP asked.

"Normally, I would say absolutely, but this friend is a bit skittish about strangers." He hated to lie to JP, but he knew that, for numerous reasons, he could not take him to where he was going.

"Okay, Gramps. I'm kind of tired anyway after the long week of classes. I'm looking forward to a good night's sleep. Thanks for dinner. You never cease to amaze me with your many talents."

"Oh, you're quite welcome. You're always welcome to visit anytime. Maybe next time that young lady friend of yours might be able to join us, too."

"Maybe so, Grandpa. Have a good night."

JP headed out the door and off to his apartment. His grandfather quickly put on his coat, grabbed his old little black bag and headed out to his car with some urgency in his steps. He knew it was going to be a long night, one he wouldn't enjoy.

5

JP'S GRANDFATHER, DR. PATRICK, was deep in thought as he drove to the safe house. Although he looked like he was only sixty, he was getting old, too old to be running around at night in secret. He knew his brain was still sharp, but physically he also knew that age was catching up to him.

The news he had received over the phone had shaken him tremendously. As he drove, he began wondering if it was all worth it. Up to this point, the cost to his people had been negligible. Tonight's raid had been different. He and his team had known the risks were high, but all had thought the target was worth it. He had known several individuals throughout his lifetime who had had OCD and with treatment had led very productive lives. They had received word that this young lady was bright and well educated, and the decision had been made. He would just have to live with the consequences.

However, the loss of William hurt for more than the obvious reasons. He had known William's parents for a long time. They had grown up with his own children and had also attended the same parish church. When William had joined the Underground, he had become like a grandson to Dr. Patrick. He did not relish having to tell William's parents the tragic news. He tried not to think about it as he continued his drive.

Dr. Patrick had led an adventurous life, but it was not just the adventure that intrigued him, it was life itself. He marveled at the complexity of life, from the smallest creature to the vastness of the universe. With all its complexity, he wondered how anyone could doubt the existence of a higher power. The mere thought that all existence came about by mere chance and evolution seemed ludicrous. Chaos existed all around, and chaos surely could not have created the beauty of life and the vastness of the night sky he could see as he looked out the moon roof of his car. It was way too simplistic an explanation for him to believe. He reasserted that he could never give up fighting for the lives of others.

The safe house was both hidden and in plain sight. He pulled into the parking lot of St. Francis of Assisi Catholic Church. It was a beautiful, old, traditional church with a tall steeple topped with a cross. The sides of the church were adorned with numerous stained-glass windows depicting scenes out of the Bible. It had once been a very vibrant parish with several thousand parishioners. However, following the global economic collapse in 2021, people had lost faith in all sectors of religion. The fact that the government began monitoring what was said from the pulpit didn't help matters. After passage of the Act, speech restrictions were placed on priests, ministers, and rabbis. Nothing derogatory could be said about the Act or, for that matter, about the government in general.

Despite all this, there were still faithful people, and some churches had remained viable. St. Francis of Assisi was one of the fortunate ones. Dr. Patrick exited his car and quickly walked to the door of the rectory that was attached to the back of the church.

He lightly knocked on the door and entered without waiting for anyone to greet him. As he entered the foyer, Father Mark met him. The priest had a grim look: his eyes were red from recent tears.

"Good evening, Dr. Patrick," he said with a slight Irish brogue.

"Good evening, Father Mark. Have William's parents been notified?" Dr. Patrick added getting right to the point.

"Aye, they have, and they should be arriving soon."

"Good. Let me know when they arrive. I will be down in the basement."

"I'll bring them down to see William when they get here."

Dr. Patrick headed down the hallway that led to the back door of the church. He passed through the door and entered the back of the church in the sacristy behind the main altar. Opening one of the closets that held the priest's many vestments, he pushed them aside and located the sliding panel that led to a set of stairs. He walked down the stairs and entered a well-lit room. Thomas was waiting for him there. He looked as if has soul had been ripped from his body.

"I'm so sorry, Dr. Patrick. I should have aborted the mission when we found out that she had already been taken from her room," Thomas said as he walked over and gave the doctor a light hug of sorrow.

"That's okay, Thomas. It's no one's fault. I'm sure William was in it all the way, and we all know the risks."

"Still, I just can't believe he's gone."

Dr. Patrick didn't really know what else to say to comfort Thomas, so, to change the subject, he asked about the patient they had saved. "How's the young lady, Thomas?"

"She's fine, Doctor. She's resting in one of the back rooms. She still seems pretty sedated. Willy's back there sitting with her."

"Does Willy know what happened to William?"

"Yes. He was here when we arrived. He took it pretty hard and cried for quite a while."

"That's too bad. I wish he hadn't seen him. I know he understands death, but I figured it would hit him hard since he and William spent a lot of time together down here. I guess sooner or later he would have to find out," Dr. Patrick added as he headed through the door to the back rooms. "I'm gonna check out our new arrival. Which room is she in?"

"Second on the left."

"Let me know when William's parents get here."

"Will do, Doctor."

Dr. Patrick entered a narrow hallway. He had been here many times before as rescued individuals passed through this safe house on their way to a new life. This particular safe house consisted of the entry room he had just left as well as four hotel-like rooms. Farther down the hall was a bathroom as well as a small kitchen. A well-hidden fire escape exited the kitchen to the outside. At the very end was a makeshift treatment operating room Dr. Patrick had used on several occasions.

He knocked lightly on the second door on the left. Willy quietly opened the door and, as usual, flashed a big smile. Willy was thirty-nine years old but had the IQ of a twelve-year-old. He was somewhat overweight, with a round face. His eyes had epicanthic folds and his slightly-opened mouth showed a thickened tongue. His hands had shortened, small fingers and only one crease on the palm. All were signs of his Down's syndrome. He had been born at a time when most Down's babies were being aborted. However, his parents had believed in the sanctity of life. His family had taken good care of him, and he had received special education until the passage of the Act, when all special-education funding was ended. It was not long after that all Down's individuals were deemed *nonproductive,* which meant a ticket to the End of Life

Care Centers. There were initially large protests over this aspect of the new Act, but it was not long before most families with Down's children had succumbed to it. Willy's parents, having seven other children to worry about, soon followed suit.

Fortunately for Willy, the newly formed Underground had selected him as their first target. They had learned of his planned termination date with the help of someone working at the hospital, and abducted him from his home without his parents' knowledge or consent. The authorities had questioned his parents at length, but were eventually convinced that they had taken no part in his disappearance.

During the past thirty years, Willy had lived in numerous safe houses and had become somewhat of an icon of the Underground movement, not only because he had been the first, but more so because of his loving and jovial personality and his ever-present desire to be of help. He had lived at his present home for several years along with Father Mark. He maintained the living quarters and helped out with anyone passing through the house.

"Hi, Dr. John," Willy said quietly.

"Hi, Willy. How's our new arrival?"

"She doing fine, Dr. John, but still sleepy."

"You keep her company for now, Willy, and I'll come back and talk to her."

"Okay, boss," Willy said with a smile as he turned back into the room.

Dr. Patrick closed the door and headed back out to the entry room.

Thomas was sitting on the couch, and the stress of the past several hours showed on his face. Dr. Patrick went over and sat beside him.

"How is she doing, Doctor?" Thomas asked, trying to sound as upbeat as possible given the circumstances.

"She's still asleep, but Willy is keeping a close eye on her. You know what a mother hen he is to our new arrivals. Why don't you go home and get some sleep, too. You look like you could use it. I'm gonna stay here and check out our patient and talk to William's parents when they arrive."

"I think I should stay and talk to them, too."

"I know you do, but you can talk to them later when you're more up to it. I'll pass on your condolences for now. Listen, Thomas. You did nothing wrong. Go home. Get some sleep."

Thomas reluctantly headed up the stairs.

William's parents arrived a short time later and were escorted down to the basement by Father Mark. Dr. Patrick showed them into the room where William's body had been placed. His mother instantly broke down and was comforted by her husband and Father Mark. Once she regained her composure, she too asked how the young lady her son had helped rescue was doing.

"She's still sleeping at the moment." Dr. Patrick replied. "They had sedated her fairly heavily before they began her trip to the morgue."

The mother winced on hearing the word *morgue,* and Dr. Patrick instantly regretted using it, since the safe house now seemed every bit like one with William lying dead in front of them. Again, he had doubts about their whole operation. At the present moment, with William's parents standing beside his body, it didn't seem at all worthwhile.

"May I see her?" his mother suddenly asked.

"Of course," Dr. Patrick replied.

She and Dr. Patrick left the room while William's father remained with him. They knocked on her door and again Willy answered. Upon seeing William's mother he stepped out of the room and gave her a long hug. Despite his Down's syndrome, he always had a way with people.

"I sorry for William," he said with a tear running down his cheek. "He was my friend."

"I know, Willy. He talked about you all the time. You were a great friend to William."

He hugged her again for a long time, then turned around and reentered the room. William's mother stood silently looking at the young lady in the room and quietly said a prayer for her. They then returned to William's room and Father Mark said some prayers with them. Dr. Patrick stood back and prayed along silently.

When they returned to the entry room, Dr. Patrick and Father Mark discussed cremation and burial plans. His parents would have liked to have had a regular funeral, but they knew that would not be possible because of William's involvement in the raid. His body would be cremated to destroy any evidence that he had been shot, and fake accident papers would be obtained so his parents would not be punished for his involvement.

It was after one in the morning before William's parents left. They knew Dr. Patrick and Father Mark would take care of the required arrangements. Dr. Patrick was tired, but he wanted to examine and talk to their new arrival before he returned home. He again headed to her room and just as he was about to knock, Willy opened the door.

"Dr. John, she waking up."

Dr. Patrick entered the room and pulled up a chair next to the bed. The room was dim but had a comforting décor. The young lady had her hands clasped tightly together in front of her chest and was anxiously looking around the room.

"Ms. Johnson, I'm Dr. Patrick. You're safe here. Do you remember what happened last night?"

She remained quiet and began rubbing her hand across her lips as though she were trying to get something off of them.

"You were at the hospital last night," Dr. Patrick continued, "and you were on your way to the End of Life Care Center. We are part of the Medical Underground, and two of our people were sent to rescue you. Can you tell me anything you remember?"

Again she remained quiet, but she had stopped rubbing her lips. She then said, "Am I dead? Is this heaven?"

"No, no, young lady. As I said, we rescued you on your way to the termination center."

After several minutes she again began rubbing her hands together and then mumbled, "Thank you, but why me?"

"Well, that's a good question. We obviously aren't able to save everyone, and who does get chosen is a complicated process. Just be thankful now that you were one of them. When you're feeling better, we can talk more about that. Right now I'd like to examine you and talk to you a little about your OCD that put you in the hospital in the first place. How long have you had a problem with it?"

"Are you talking about things like rubbing my hands together and rubbing my lips together?"

"Yes. You've been diagnosed as having what's called obsessive compulsive disorder. Were you unaware of what's been bothering you?"

"I knew something was wrong with me, but I was too embarrassed to talk to anyone about it."

"Well, as it turns out, it's probably good you didn't. Can you tell me a little bit about how it affected you?"

Her face turned a little red, and she looked away.

"It's okay if you aren't ready. But in order to help you, we will need to understand a little more about it."

"I know. I've been hiding it for so many years, it's very difficult to talk about it."

"Okay, then. If you agree I'll go ahead and start you on some medicine that should help."

"Okay," she said hesitantly.

He then started her on some Anafranil and told her that one of the psychiatrists from the Underground would be by in the next few days to talk to her some more about her problem. He then introduced her to Willy and Father Mark and told her they would be helping her out while here at this particular safe house. Finally, at about four o'clock in the morning, he went to his car and headed home. Yes, he was really getting too old for all this.

6

JP ENTERED HIS APARTMENT and crashed on his couch, suffering from a food coma from the dinner his grandfather had made for him. Dr. Patrick's sudden exit seemed a little strange to JP, even for his grandpa.

Before going to bed he remembered he and his dad were playing phone tag. His concern for his grandfather gave JP one more reason to try and reach his father again.

The phone rang. His dad answered, "Hello?"

"Hey, Dad. Is this a bad time?" JP asked his father.

"Never for my boy. Sorry I haven't returned your call from yesterday, I just finished a sixteen-hour shift. Never a free moment in the Ministry."

"That's okay. I actually was just leaving a probability class when I called you, so we probably would not have much time to talk anyway."

"Gotcha. So what's on your mind?

"Nothing much. I just finished having dinner with Grandpa."

"Really? How is the old fart?"

"That's what I was calling to ask you. Have you spoken to him lately? He seems kind of stressed out."

"Stressed? How stressed can a retired doctor be? Too much golf?"

"Seriously, Dad. He seems worn out, but maybe it's just me."

"He is getting old, son. That's how old people are. He'll be fine. He always is."

"If you say so, Dad."

"How is school going? Seems like forever ago to me that I was in there. It's important that you stick to your studies. You'll make a fine addition to the Ministry."

"Yes, Dad. I know. School is going well."

"And Sam?" his father had asked playfully.

"Still a friend Dad. We were both in class last week and were visited by some folks from the Ministry."

"Interesting. What was the topic of discussion?"

"Obsessive compulsive disorder."

"And its negligible treatment result," JP's father blurted out. "It all comes down to *quality*, not the *quantity*, of care. Help those with a treatment that really advances their life, son. And recognize those that can't be helped."

"I get all that. But Dad, this girl was terrified. She sat motionless in class. Didn't speak at all. Just sat there. Zoned out. Crying."

"OCD is embarrassing to those living with it. Hiding in plain sight for years and being caught. It's a daily shame, son."

"It was more than that. She was terrified. I imagine I would be frightened as well with two armed guards hovering over me in front of a class of strangers talking about my inability to curtail my OCD."

"Those guards were there for her protection. And yours too, buddy."

JP couldn't help but question that. "She was tied down to a

wheelchair, Dad. What could have happened?"

"Well, there are people out there who feel differently than you and I do, son. Look, there will forever be an opposition to any system. People could threaten a higher learning facility in an effort to prove their opposition. It's very simple, JP. We treat who we are told to treat, after careful consideration to all the factors. This is what you're learning. The system works. The system is constantly being evaluated and evolving, but it is working."

"Didn't seem to be working for that girl."

"We treat the majority, to protect the whole. That's the *Cliff's Notes* version of your class."

"And the armed guards?"

"That's why we have the MEU, son. Let them deal with the sympathizers. You learn to treat the people who will be forever thankful for your help. Making the most difference you can in this life."

"Okay. I get it," JP relented.

"Listen, son, I need to get as much rest as I can before the next call from the hospital."

"Okay, Dad, I'll let you go."

"Say hi to your grandfather for me. And JP, I love you."

"Love you too, Dad. Get some rest."

7

CAPTAIN JAMESON WAS LIVID that a patient had been snatched from under their noses. It was bad for the healthcare system—and his reputation. He also knew he would have to answer to Minister Atherton. He didn't want to get on his bad side, especially right after meeting his lovely daughter.

After leaving the dinner, Jameson had gone back to his office to wait for Lieutenant Osgood. He wanted to hear firsthand what had gone down at the pharmacy. He would then talk to the officers on duty at the End of Life Care Center and the hospital. Someone's head was gonna roll, and it was certainly not going to be his.

Lieutenant Osgood reported to the captain's office as ordered. He debriefed him with what little there was to tell. He knew the captain was not pleased with the events of the evening, but he believed everything had been done by the book.

"Did you find any evidence at the scene to give us some direction in the investigation?"

"No, sir. The building was clean. We talked to the owner and the only pertinent thing he could tell us was that there were two men in the pharmacy two days ago who said they were from the security company. They had told him they were there to just check the equipment, and unfortunately, he didn't question them. He was able to give us a description, but it was pretty vague. We'll have forensics see if they can get any prints off the security system, but I have my doubts."

"Also have the pharmacy owner watch some of the security videos from the hospital to see if they were the same two guys that took the young woman from the tunnel. Now have the security officer from the hospital come in."

The officer recounted what had happened at the front entrance of the hospital, including the fact that he believed he may have shot one of the individuals as they were driving away.

"What makes you think you hit one of them? Did you actually see one of them get hit, or was there any blood at the scene?"

"Uh, no, sir. I just thought that I may have hit one through the van. There were two in the back and two in the front."

"Great!" the captain shouted. "Why don't we just go check the morgue right now because with that kind of proof, I'm sure as hell he'll be there!" He turned his back to the young officer and stared out the window.

The young officer sheepishly looked over at the lieutenant with eyes pleading for some reassurance.

"Roger, go on out and file your report," the lieutenant said. "I'll talk to you some more tomorrow."

The young officer glanced back at the captain who continued to stare at the window with his back turned. He then glanced at the lieutenant who nodded for him to leave.

"Anything else, Captain?" the lieutenant added after the young officer had left.

"Actually, it probably would be worthwhile to check around

to see if any of the surrounding emergency rooms have recently had patients with injuries consistent with gunshot wounds. I know it's a long shot, but you never know."

"Will do, Captain," Lieutenant Osgood replied, smiling to himself as he exited the office.

The captain sat down at his desk and reviewed the evening in his mind. Something wasn't adding up. He still wondered about the lieutenant, although he seemed like a good man. *He had been here before I arrived,* he thought, *and he just seemed unfazed by the evening's events, almost like he was happy about the outcome. He will definitely need watching.*

8

DR. ATHERTON WAS IN his office bright and early the next morning. The director's office was very spacious, befitting the power that was wielded from it. Numerous framed diplomas and certificates covered one of the walls. He had heard of the events of the previous evening and was disturbed about the whole situation, but was waiting for Captain Jameson to give him a full report. He wanted to hear all the facts before passing judgment on anyone in particular. He was also interested in what had transpired between the captain and his daughter. He knew that she wouldn't divulge much, but the captain might, especially if he thought he was in hot water.

He was now debating if it had been a good idea to introduce the two. Sam was his only daughter, and he truly wanted the best for her. He believed that the captain was a good man—albeit ambitious. Perhaps if they did start seeing each other, it would be a good way to keep an eye on both of them.

As expected, Captain Jameson arrived precisely on time at eight. Dr. Atherton ushered him into his office and shut the door.

"What can you tell me about last night? I've heard the gist of what went down, but I'd like to hear the details and know what you're doing about the whole situation. Might I add that you came to us with high recommendations, so I'm a little surprised to hear that this happened on your watch."

"Yes, sir, I am sorry about this whole situation and, trust me, I take full responsibility for it."

He filled the minister in on what little he knew at this time, including the fact that his officer at the hospital thought he might have shot one of the kidnappers as they were pulling away from the scene.

Although he knew what the answer would be, the minister asked, "Any reports from surrounding emergency departments about any unexplained gunshot wounds?"

"Nothing at this time, sir," the captain replied, thinking to himself that he was thankful he ordered the lieutenant to check the surrounding emergency rooms. "However, I'm sure they would try to avoid that unless absolutely necessary. We'll keep looking. Sooner or later, we'll get a break, and we'll close the local operation down. I just can't understand why they keep persisting. These people they're trying to help probably don't even want to be helped."

"Do you really think that's true?" Dr. Atherton replied.

"I know in my mother's case, I would have been very happy if someone would have been able to end her suffering sooner."

"I was unaware you had such a personal interest in this matter. Do you think your mother felt the same way?" Dr. Atherton knew the captain was passionate about his work but had never known why. It never hurt to know an individual's motivation.

"I don't know for sure, but I can't imagine she wanted to continue suffering. I was pretty young so I really never asked her, and I doubt she would have told me anyway."

"Perhaps she enjoyed having a little extra time with you."

This statement caught the captain off guard, and he wasn't

quite sure where this conversation was leading. Perhaps the minister was testing him to see if he was truly committed to his job as commander of the Medical Enforcement Unit.

"I have no idea, sir, but getting back to last night, I have the pharmacy owner going over the hospital security videos. We've also contacted local police to help keep an eye out for these men. I'll keep you up to date." Anxious to end this conversation, he added, "Is that all, sir?"

"Well, actually there is one other matter. I noticed you and Sam seemed to be hitting it off last night."

Captain Jameson again was caught off guard. "Yes, sir. She seems lovely. I hope you didn't mind my monopolizing her time last night. I'm afraid I'm not too comfortable at parties like the one last night. Your daughter was a pleasant distraction."

"No, not at all. I imagine she would've rather been elsewhere last night, also. I'm sure she just went as a favor to me. I'm glad she had you there. I hope she didn't bore you with stories about how hard she's having to work in school."

"No, sir. We had a nice conversation. She really is a delightful woman," the captain repeated, hoping to score some points with the minister.

"Thank you, Captain. She's a lot like her mother used to be, beautiful and bull-headed. Therefore, you should watch yourself. Also—don't forget—she's got a lot of studying so she does well in school."

"I will not forget, sir," the captain replied as he headed to the door. The minister's comments seemed to imply that he had no problem with him seeing his daughter as long as she had time to study. Things were looking a little brighter than they had just a short time ago. Certainly dating the daughter of the Minister of Health couldn't hurt his professional climb.

9

ABOUT A MONTH HAD passed since JP's dinner with his grandfather. It had been a revealing evening. He hoped he would be able to get back over to see him again soon, perhaps over the winter break. He'd have to get through exams first. JP thought it would be nice to hear some more stories about what surgery was like back before decisions were made by the government. He couldn't imagine having the authority to make decisions for patients without worrying about statistics and probability, or who was watching over your shoulder.

JP had been spending most of his time studying in the library. Unfortunately, he had seen little of Sam outside the classroom. They had chatted between classes, but for the most part she seemed to be distracted and unusually busy. In class, she didn't seem to be as sharp. At times he noticed her staring off into space while twirling her hair with her fingers.

The opportunity to find out what was going on with Sam came one night at the library. JP had been studying for a couple of hours and decided to take a break. He headed to the student lounge to get a drink. As he walked in he saw Sam talking to a slightly older man who was well groomed and dressed in a suit. He walked over to where they were sitting and greeted Sam.

"Hey, Sam."

"Hi, JP."

"Is this where you've been hanging out in the evenings lately? I haven't seen you up in the library much."

"I've been doing most of my studying at home lately."

The captain cleared his throat and stood.

"Oh, I'm sorry. JP, this is Mike Jameson. He works at the Ministry. Daddy introduced us at the dinner they held several weeks ago."

"Nice to meet you, Mike," JP said reaching out to shake his hand. "I'm one of Sam's classmates and was a study partner, but lately she hasn't been around much."

"I'm afraid I'm partly to blame for that. I've been taking up quite a bit of her time since her father introduced us."

"Oh, of course. I was concerned about her, though, since she hasn't been to the library much lately."

"Rest assured, she's putting in her share of studying. I practically had to swear on a stack of Bibles to her father that I wouldn't interfere with her education."

JP noticed Sam blush. He also felt a pang of sadness. It was obvious now why Sam had been so distracted; the reason was standing right in front of him.

"Are you a doctor?" JP asked.

"No, no. I'm just a bureaucrat who answers to Sam's father. I leave the doctoring to those much smarter than me."

"Well, any friend of Sam's is a friend of mine. I guess I'd better get back to the books. It was nice meeting you, Mike. See ya in class, Sam."

JP turned and headed toward the coffee machine, then turned

back toward Sam.

"Oh, by the way, Sam, what are you doing over winter break? I'd still like to have you meet my grandfather. He's a very interesting character."

"I'd like to, JP, but Mike and I are going skiing. Maybe I can meet him after break."

"Sounds great. I'll see you guys later."

JP got a cup of coffee and headed back to the library, thinking all the while what might have been if he hadn't waited too long to pursue Sam on a different level. At least she seemed to have met a nice man. He hoped she was still putting in some time studying. Even with her father being the Minister of Health, she still had to pass all the exams.

Captain Jameson noticed Sam watching JP as he headed out the door.

"Have you guys been more than good friends?"

"No, no. I did think it could have led to something at one time, but that was before you came along," she said with a slight grin. "He is a good friend, though, and I would like to meet his grandfather. He sounds like an engaging man. JP talks about him all the time. I hear he was quite an adventurous man before settling down as a surgeon. He's apparently eighty now, but still very active."

"Sounds like my kind of man," Mike replied. "Maybe I can meet him some day, too."

"I'm sure JP would like that. Well, as JP said, I better get back to the books or I won't be around school much longer, and I don't think Daddy would like that."

"Nor would I," the captain said as he bent over and kissed her on the top of the head.

10

LIEUTENANT OSGOOD HAD BEEN with the MEU for more than ten years. It was a good job, one that many in law enforcement would love to have. It had good benefits—federal benefits. He had made the jump from civil police work to the MEU for that very reason. He was married and had five children, and his family meant everything to him. His job meant security, not so much for him, but for his family.

He had worked hard and quickly moved up in the ranks due to his integrity, diligence and good police work. There was only one problem. Although he enjoyed the police aspect of his job, his heart was not truly behind the MEU's mission. As long as he kept his mind off the fact that people were being killed in the End of Life Center, he could justify doing his job to support his family. After all, his job was just to enforce the law. He didn't make the law, and luckily he didn't have to decide who lived and who died.

His previous captain had been a good man and basically allowed him to run the unit. Unfortunately, things were different now. Captain Jameson was a hands-on commander controlling all aspects of the day-to-day operations of the unit. The captain had handpicked most of the men on the special details. Osgood felt like his boss didn't trust him and, worse yet, that he was closely watched. Perhaps it was paranoia, but he even thought he might be having him followed at times.

The events of the raid on the End of Life Care Center a few weeks prior had not helped matters. Lieutenant Osgood knew the captain had been embarrassed by the whole event and had probably received an ass-chewing from the Minister of Health. Osgood worried that he would be demoted or worse.

He was on his way home from work, and was trying to put all of this out of his mind. He tried not take his work home with him. He knew too many cops whose marriages had fallen apart because they couldn't separate work from family. Home to him was his little paradise. His wife and kids made life worthwhile.

Osgood pulled into his drive, and his two youngest children came running out of their modest home. Their youngest was just three and a bruiser of a little boy. Katie, who had just turned five, came running out with him. She was his little princess, the only girl of the five children. She jumped into his arms, and he carried her into the house with his youngest running alongside.

The lieutenant entered the kitchen where his wife, Janet, was preparing dinner, and he instantly knew something was wrong. He could tell Janet had been crying and was now still holding back tears. He put Katie down, and Janet walked over and hugged him tightly and started sobbing. A minute later she regained her composure.

"What is it, dear?" the lieutenant calmly asked.

"It's Katie. She had her preschool physical last week, and they drew some blood. The pediatrician's office called early this morning and said the results of her blood count were concerning. They asked if I could come in so I went there this afternoon." She again started to cry.

The lieutenant guided her to a chair and helped her sit down. He sat down beside her and waited for her to start talking again. Katie came running back into the kitchen at that point.

"Daddy, what's wrong with Mommy?"

"She's okay, honey. You go back in and play with the boys."

"Okay, Daddy. But make Mommy be happy again."

"I will, honey. Now run and play."

Katie left the kitchen, and the lieutenant looked back at his wife. As their eyes met, she said, "The pediatrician said she's in the early stage of leukemia."

"What do you mean? Blood cancer? What did they say?"

Lieutenant Osgood's heart raced and he started to sweat.

"Did he say exactly what that meant? Will she need to get treatment started soon?"

Just as his wife started to answer, Katie again came back into the kitchen. "Mommy, we're hungry."

"Okay, honey. You go back and tell the boys that dinner will be ready soon." Katie skipped back out of the kitchen.

"Maybe they just made a mistake. She doesn't even look sick."

"I know. That's what I said, also. But they assured me there was no mistake."

"So what happens now?"

"The doctor said it depends on her type of leukemia. She has to have a bone marrow biopsy first. The government has approved treatment for some types of leukemia, but not all. He said he can tell us more once the biopsy is done."

The lieutenant knew what was implied. No treatment meant a trip to the End of Life Care Center. He also knew that was never going to happen to his little princess. He would find a way at whatever cost, no matter where he worked.

11

JP WAS QUITE HAPPY that winter break was almost here. Not having Sam to study with had taken what little enjoyment there was out of all the arduous studying every night. Also, ever since his dinner with his grandfather a couple months ago, his focus seemed to be off. It was as if he wanted to learn the kind of medicine his grandfather had known, not the world in which statistics and bureaucracy made the decisions for him. JP looked forward to visiting his grandfather again. He had hoped Sam would go with him but all her free time now was being spent with the new man JP had met in the library break room.

After hearing about the Hippocratic Oath his grandfather had taken when he graduated from medical school, JP had decided to attend the mid-year graduation ceremony. Several students had been unable to graduate on time earlier in the year for various reasons such as having to repeat rotations or classes, or because of illness. Therefore the school was holding an extra graduation ceremony for them at the end of the fall semester. It was going to be a small group without the usual pomp and circumstance, but he thought he would see if they took any kind of oath.

He sat in the back of the auditorium and watched as the graduating students marched in. Surprisingly, they were actually wearing caps and gowns, and there were only seven of them. Once everyone was seated, there was a brief introduction by the dean of the school followed by a short talk from Sam's father, who was representing the Ministry. The students then marched across the stage and received their diplomas. This ceremony was followed by a brief congratulatory talk from another faculty member. The graduates were then asked to rise from their seats and JP thought they were going to start marching out. He stood up to get out before them, but then he heard the dean ask the students to raise their right hand for the oath. What followed bore no resemblance to what JP had read on his grandfather's wall.

Wherefore I have been trained in the mathematical and healing arts, it is my duty to righteously carry out said arts to the best of my ability.

Whereas I have learned that the greater good is greater than the individual good, it is my duty to follow the ordinances of the government in the execution of health care to all.

Although it may be profitable to treat individuals outside the premises of approved centers, I will forgo such endeavors or risk forfeiture of my license.

Whereas the treatment of terminally ill patients is harmful for the good of the patient and society, I will forgo useless prolongation of life.

Whereas some individuals are a liability to society, I will not hesitate to prescribe termination when necessary, according to accepted ordinances.

Whereas the government has a right to the medical

records of all citizens, I will divulge all patient information to the Ministry of Health, in accordance with The Medical Reconciliation Act.

To these I swear before my fellow practitioners and the State.

Following the oath, the small audience erupted in applause. As JP headed toward the exit, he grabbed a program for the event. On the back page he found a copy of the oath the students had just recited. It was indeed entitled *The Kevorkian Oath.*

※ ※ ※

After leaving the graduation ceremony, JP headed over to his grandfather's house. He was looking forward to a few days with him. The fall semester had been grueling and he was tired of studying every free moment. A little rest and relaxation with his grandpa was just what he needed.

It was a beautiful early-winter evening, which made the ride even more enjoyable. However, his thoughts soon drifted back to the ceremony he had just witnessed. It amazed him how medicine had changed in such a short time. What he was being taught bore no resemblance to what his grandfather had practiced. The Kevorkian Oath sounded like something out of a horror movie compared to the Hippocratic Oath he had read a few months before. The more he thought about it, the more he wondered if he belonged in medicine. Perhaps he had made a big mistake. He was anxious to talk to his grandfather about his feelings.

A short time later, he arrived at his grandfather's house. He had been in such deep thought that he actually couldn't remember part of the drive. At least he had arrived safely and hadn't hurt anyone on the way.

As usual, his grandfather greeted him at the door with a big smile. Instantly, JP's spirits were lifted.

"Good evening. Good evening. Come on in. I thought you were going to be here a little earlier."

JP walked in saying, "Well, I discovered that there was an interim graduation this evening so I thought I'd drop by and see if they said the Hippocratic Oath or something different."

They sat down in the living room. His grandfather already knew the answer, but asked, "What did you find out?"

"It was disgusting. They recited the Kevorkian Oath and it's nothing like the Hippocratic Oath. Now I see why you have that one framed on the wall. I'm still haunted by that young lady who was paraded before the class a few months ago, and now hearing that oath makes me wonder if I'm cut out to be a doctor. I just don't know if I could send somebody to the End of Life Care Center if I thought they could be cured."

Dr. Patrick liked what he was hearing his grandson say, but it was obvious that he needed to tread lightly. He wanted to empathize with JP without discouraging him from completing his education. "You know, JP, doctors nowadays do have to do things they don't want to do. On the other hand, they also do a lot of good for many people. Before the Act was passed, doctors and pharmacists had lost some of their independence. They were forced to do procedures and dispense drugs that were against their conscience. It was just one of the many steps that led up to the Act. Despite that, we did the best we could and just had to ask God to forgive whatever we weren't able to avoid. I imagine your dad is doing the same thing now."

"He is. I talked to him recently and he is definitely going along with the program. Talking to him didn't seem to allay my concerns," JP said with a somber look on his face.

"I'd still like to hear more about what it was like working

back before the Act."

"What do you say we get some food in your stomach first? After that, I'll lighten the evening up with a few yarns from the old days."

"Sounds good, Grandpa. I could use something to take my mind off what's going on now."

Dinner was again superb and JP marveled at what his grandfather was able to accomplish at his age. Following dinner, they retired to the living room and his grandfather lit up a pipe that filled the room with an aromatic odor. It reminded JP of burning wood in an open fire, along with a hint of wintergreen. Grandpa offered JP a little Glenlivet Scotch and regaled him with many more adventurous tales of his youth—tales of danger, beautiful women, and world travel. However, as the evening wore on, JP's thoughts again returned to their earlier discussion about his medical training.

"Grandpa, do you really think that doctors can make a difference now or are they just pawns of the government?"

"That's a good question. But of course I think we can still make a difference and in more ways than you might imagine. I don't think all people fully agree with what has happened to the health care system. When the Act first went into effect, there were countless protests. And some people still object. I'm sure you are aware that there are some that do more than just talk."

"Yeah, I've heard about people who rescue people from the End of Life Care Center. It's hard to imagine they're doing much good. After all, what's one life compared to all those not being treated or terminated?"

"Well, let me tell you a little story told to me many years ago; one I've never forgotten. It should give you a little perspective. There was a bad storm along the coast one night, with strong winds and huge waves. The next morning, a young man was walking along the beach and saw thousands of starfish lying on the sand. As he walked along, he came upon an elderly man who was tossing a starfish back into the water. As he approached the man, he asked, 'Why are you doing that? There are thousands of these starfish on the beach. You're not going to make a difference.' The elderly man bent over, picked up another starfish, and tossed it back into the ocean. He then looked at the young man, and said, 'I made a difference for that one.' Now do you understand why some people still feel like they can make a difference?"

"I guess so, but it still seems like a hopeless and uphill battle to me."

Dr. Patrick contemplated telling JP about his role in the Underground, but he wasn't sure if it was safe or appropriate. He thought JP would understand, and even hoped he would be enthusiastic about it, but he wasn't convinced. He would sleep on it and decide tomorrow.

"Well, all this chatter and good scotch has made me sleepy. Why don't you bunk out here and go to church with me in the morning?"

"Do they still have daily Mass somewhere?"

"Of course. I'm sure Father Mark at St. Francis of Assisi would love to meet you. He's been a friend of mine for some time."

"Well, I came over here for a little R and R. I think I might just enjoy doing that with you."

"That's great. You can bunk down in the spare bedroom. Mass is at eight and we can grab some breakfast afterwards. Father Mark is always up for a good meal and might even be able to join us. Perhaps he can add some insight into your schooling issues."

"Perhaps," JP responded somewhat skeptically as he headed to the spare bedroom. "Good night."

"Good night, JP. I've got a couple calls to make, then I'll be heading to bed also."

✻ ✻ ✻

Dr. Patrick called Father Mark to tell him he would be bringing his grandson to Mass in the morning. He asked Father Mark to join them for breakfast afterwards. The priest said he would love to. They chatted a couple more minutes and then Dr. Patrick placed an additional call. The gentleman who answered gave a warm greeting once he knew who was calling. Dr. Patrick discussed his conversation with JP with this man, who listened intently. After Dr. Patrick had filled him in, the man agreed that introducing JP to the Underground network was probably okay, albeit somewhat risky for the organization as well as JP. However, he had known Dr. Patrick for a long time and trusted his instincts.

Dr. Patrick hung up the phone and headed to bed, making plans for the next day.

12

LIEUTENANT OSGOOD AND HIS wife were dreading the appointment with the pediatrician. There was still the possibility that the results of the tests would reveal Katie had treatable leukemia. Yet they both had a sick feeling in their stomachs that things would not go well today. The office was cold and unappealing to both adults and children. Gone were the days when pediatricians decorated their offices with cute pictures, aquariums, and playrooms. It was strictly business.

They checked in with the receptionist, who was just as cold as the décor. She wore a bland, colored smock with no cute little characters. No eye contact was made during the entire registration and they were then instructed to take a seat. The lieutenant did his best to keep Katie entertained. They had brought a couple of books with them and he held her on his lap and read to her. She giggled when he made animal noises as she saw the animals in the books. Twenty minutes later, they were escorted into a small exam room. It was dim and Lieutenant Osgood thought the temperature had to be colder than in the waiting room. He picked

Katie up and sat her on his lap to keep her warm.

About fifteen minutes later, the doctor walked in without a smile or greeting and sat with his computer tablet. He began clicking through Katie's file. Finally, after several minutes, he looked up and said, "It looks like we have a problem."

The lieutenant's heart sank and his wife put her head down and started crying. The lieutenant felt like punching the emotionless talking head in front of him and he probably would have, had it not been for Katie's presence.

The talking head continued. "It looks like Katie's type of leukemia is treatable. However according to the Medical Reconciliation Act guidelines, the probability of success is suboptimal and the cost is prohibitive. With a bone marrow transplant we're looking at two hundred fifty thousand dollars."

"Is that it? We just give up, like she's some pet dog?"

"I'm afraid so," he replied without a hint of emotion on his face. "We are not allowed to treat her."

In one swift move, JP handed Katie to his wife, jumped to his feet and grabbed the doctor by the collar of his white coat. "You son of a bitch! What kind of doctor are you? I've seen more compassion from a vet than you."

"Sir, kindly remove your hands or I will have to call the MEU and have you escorted out."

"I am the Medical Enforcement Unit, you idiot," the lieutenant shouted as he let go of the doctor. He looked at his wife who was almost sobbing as she hugged Katie tightly. "Let's go, honey. We'll find a real doctor who actually has a heart."

The doctor had a near-gloating look on his face. "Unfortunately, that won't help you," he said. "No doctor will be allowed to treat her no matter where you take her. In fact, you need to wait here while we make an appointment for her at the End of Life Care Center."

At that the lieutenant swung his fist at the doctor, stopping just short of striking his face. The doctor cowered back and then quickly ran out the door. The lieutenant helped his wife and Katie up and followed the doctor out of the exam room. He did not follow the doctor's order, and instead they walked straight out the door.

Once inside their car, the lieutenant grabbed the steering wheel with both hands and leaned his head against it. He needed to calm down and think through this. *There has to be another answer.* His daughter was not going to be treated like a sick animal, at least not if he had anything to say about it.

After several minutes, his wife said, "What are we going to do, Jaye?"

"I don't know, honey. I just need some time to think. Let's get out of here and head home. We'll think of something." As he drove, the lieutenant's mind raced. He wondered if they could hide Katie and find her treatment. But he obviously had to think about the boys and his wife, too. If he didn't comply with the doctor's orders he would surely be fired and jailed, his family's financial security ruined. He kept looking out his rear view mirror, wondering if they were being followed.

13

DR. ATHERTON TRULY ENJOYED golf. Unlike many sports where you were part of a team, in golf it was you against the course. When played by the rules, golf taught honesty, patience, integrity, determination, and kindness. But the game could also bring out the worst in people because its rules were largely built upon an honor system. Dr. Atherton was just finishing the fifteenth hole and was having a great round. The weather was perfect, seventy degrees with crystal clear blue skies and no wind. The golf gods were truly watching over him today. He was on pace to break eighty for the first time in his life. He could already start to feel the muscles in his body tighten up as he headed over to the sixteenth tee box. His playing partners were all bemoaning the fact that he was kicking their butts and was going to walk away with their friendly wager.

As he started up to the tee box, his cell phone rang. He considered not answering it, but in his position as Minister of Health, he knew he had no choice. He waved his playing companions on, stepped back off the tee box, and answered, "Hello, this is Dr.

Atherton. May I help you?"

"I'm sorry to bother you, sir. This is Lieutenant Osgood with the Medical Enforcement Unit. Something's come up and I was wondering if you could meet with me as soon as possible."

"Yes, I know who you are, Lieutenant. Is it something about the enforcement unit?"

"No, sir. This is personal."

"Can it wait about forty-five minutes?"

"That would be fine, sir. Shall we meet in your office, sir?"

"That's fine, but we'd better make it about an hour and an half then, since I'm about a half-hour out of town."

"Thank you, sir. I'll see you there in an hour and a half."

Dr. Atherton hung up his cell phone and headed back to the sixteenth tee box with a puzzled expression on his face. He couldn't imagine what was bothering the lieutenant. He knew there had been some tension between him and Captain Jameson, so perhaps things had come to a head between them.

With his mind still on the lieutenant, he stepped back onto the sixteenth tee and hooked it out of bounds. So much for breaking eighty. His buddies were now smiling. Golf was truly a game of concentration, and frustration.

After finishing with an eighty-four for his round, Dr. Atherton headed back to his office. He thought the lieutenant was a good man and couldn't quite understand why Captain Jameson didn't trust him. Although the captain had not handpicked Osgood for his team, there was nothing in his file to suggest that he was not loyal to the MEU.

The drive back to his office was otherwise peaceful. His thoughts drifted to his daughter, Samantha. She was doing reasonably well in medical school, despite her initial desire to pursue another career. However, her developing relationship with Captain Jameson worried him a little. Jameson was somewhat older than Sam and Dr. Atherton wondered if she just wasn't caught up in the nature of his job. She had always thought the MEU was the coolest part of the Ministry of Health, despite her father's efforts to show her the many other functions of the Ministry.

When Atherton arrived at his office, Lieutenant Osgood was waiting. He seemed very agitated and his face looked more strained than Dr. Atherton had ever seen it. The lieutenant had always been very calm and collected even under tense circumstances.

"Come on in, Lieutenant," Dr. Atherton said as he entered his office. "What's on your mind, Jaye?"

The lieutenant sat down like he was carrying a five hundred-pound weight on his shoulders. He initially seemed at a loss for words but slowly began. "It's my daughter, sir, my only daughter, Katie. We just found out that she has leukemia."

Dr. Atherton quickly realized why the lieutenant had asked for the meeting. This was not at all what he had expected. "Have they determined the type of leukemia she has? Many of them are treatable nowadays."

"That's the problem, sir. Today, we met with this bureaucratic ass—I'm sorry, sir—robot of a pediatrician who said that although it could be treated, the probability of success was low and the cost was prohibitive. My wife and I just don't know what to do. We just can't sit back and let them take her to the End of Life Care Center. She's only five, sir! There's got to be another way. We didn't know where else to turn, sir." The moment he'd gotten the words out, the lieutenant began sobbing into his hands.

"I'm sorry, Jaye," said Dr. Atherton. "I know your daughter means everything to you. I'm just not sure there's anything I can do. The Act applies to everyone, even the politicians themselves."

"I seriously doubt it applies to everyone."

"Everyone, Jaye. Everyone. Years ago, there was a brilliant

doctor who attended Stanford and then went on to run a series of clinics. He became a big advocate for the Act, doing media interviews and espousing its virtues. This doctor, his name was Eric Blumsfield, had a form of treatable pancreatic cancer, but the Act deemed the treatment success rate too low. Blumsfield didn't run; he didn't seek underground treatment. He didn't try to pull strings. He followed protocol. He understood that a greater good was being served. This has come to be known as the Blumsfield rule. No exceptions!"

"But this doctor with cancer wasn't a five-year-old, sir, a young innocent child who does have at least a chance to survive according to the statistics. There has to be another option," the lieutenant pleaded. "What if we took her to another country?"

"That would not work for two reasons. One, now that her diagnosis is in the system, she would be unable to get a passport. And two, most other countries had some variation of the Medical Reconciliation Act long before we did."

"This is bullshit!" The words slipped from Osgood's mouth.

"Bullshit or not, your job is to enforce the rules and equality of the MRA."

"My apologies, sir. My thoughts are focused on my daughter's health."

The lieutenant looked even more dejected as he began to exit the office. "By the way, you may be getting a report that I threatened the doctor. That would be true. I sort of lost it with that guy."

"I understand your outburst. I am a little concerned, however, that you thought I would be able to bend the rules for you on this matter. You're beginning to sound like the very people we expect you to identify and arrest. One might think that you have more in common with the Underground than you do with your department. Do I need to speak to Captain Jameson on this matter?"

"Of course not, sir. I can assure you I have no sympathy for the Underground and its members."

* * *

Osgood left the office and headed straight for home. His thoughts were still on his daughter. He felt betrayed by the people he had faithfully served. He couldn't help but wonder, would the Underground be sympathetic to Katie, the daughter of a lieutenant in the Medical Reinforcement Unit?

14

JP WASN'T SURE WHAT to expect at Mass. Although he had been raised Catholic, his parents hadn't really practiced their faith to any great extent so it was natural for him to fall away from the church. Just as in Europe, the U. S. had become quite secular and the number of churches, synagogues and mosques had significantly diminished. Many former churches were now used as warehouses, restaurants, or apartment buildings.

JP rode with his grandfather to St. Francis of Assisi church. He was a little nervous about riding with him, given his age, but he soon realized his concern was unjustified. His grandfather handled the car with ease as he whistled happily along. "Has the Mass changed any in the past several years?" JP queried.

His grandpa chuckled and said, "No, JP. The Mass has essentially been the same for over two thousand years. No government is going to change that. They may try to control what is preached, but the Mass itself is still the same. In the past, even in countries where religions were totally outlawed, secret Masses were carried out frequently. Many people lost their lives over religion. There will always be Masses and they will not change."

"Well, I guess I shouldn't be too lost today, then. It might feel good to be back in church. Maybe I can find some of my answers about my career there. Who knows, maybe a bolt of lightning will hit me," he added jokingly.

"Perhaps it will, JP," his grandfather replied. He wondered if showing JP the safe house just might be that bolt of lightning. He truly hoped JP would embrace the mission of traditional medicine. It could help him stay committed to his medical training.

They arrived at the church and JP was surprised to see the parking lot almost full. "Is it always this crowded at Mass, Grandpa?"

"Yes and in fact, sometimes there's no room in the parking lot at all."

They got out and headed to the front door of the church. JP was impressed by the sheer beauty of the building. It reminded him of some of the churches he had seen when he and a friend had toured around Europe after college. The only difference was that most of those churches had usually been empty. This church seemed alive even on the outside.

JP followed his grandfather in and they sat towards the back of the church. People were kneeling and praying and his grandfather got down and did the same. JP found himself kneeling and praying and it felt familiar.

It was like getting back on a bicycle after not riding for many years. Right away, the prayers he had learned and recited as a child came flooding back to him and then he began praying for guidance through the many choices facing him. A peaceful feeling came over him; one he had not felt in some time.

The priest entered the altar area and the Mass began. He was younger than JP had expected. JP had heard that there were fewer and fewer young men entering the priesthood. Obviously there must have been some answering the call.

The priest's homily centered around how life was given to us as a gift from God and how we as individuals should respect it and make the most of it for the good of others, not just ourselves. JP noticed that the priest avoided the subject of abortion and euthanasia. Under the Act, these subjects were taboo even for the Catholic priests who had preached against them for many decades.

Later in the Mass, his grandfather went up to receive communion, but JP stayed in his pew. He did remember that one must be free from mortal sin before receiving communion. Not attending Mass for many years rendered him unable to receive communion. As the people were returning from communion, he spotted an attractive young lady with long blond hair. She looked familiar but he was unable to place her. He made a note to himself to ask his grandfather if he knew her.

The Mass ended with a final blessing from the priest and the people slowly filed out of the church. JP noticed that the familiar young lady stayed afterward; apparently to pray. He and his grandfather left their pew and exited at the front of the church. As they walked around to the rectory, JP asked about the young lady.

"Grandpa, did you happen to notice the cute young lady with the long blond hair in church?"

"How could I not notice?" his grandfather said, chuckling to himself.

"Do you know who she is? She looks vaguely familiar to me."

"That's Emily Johns. She's been going to church here for a couple months. She is a nice sight to behold, isn't she?"

"Yes. she is, Grandpa, but aren't you just a little too old to be noticing that?"

"You're never too old to appreciate beauty, my son. Just like a nice painting or a nice classic car, beauty is beauty. Her beauty is not just skin deep either. I've met her and she is a lovely young lady."

"Well, perhaps I'd better start going to Mass more frequently," JP replied, with a sly grin on his face.

"It's not the best reason to be going to church, but I guess it would be a good start."

※ ※ ※

Father Mark met them at the entrance to the rectory, and Dr. Patrick introduced JP. The priest shook JP's hand and closed the rectory door behind him.

"It's very nice to meet the grandson of one of our most distinguished parishioners. Dr. Patrick is like one of the fixtures around here."

"It's nice to meet you, Father. Are you sure you're talking about my grandpa?" JP replied with a laugh.

"Watch it young man. I may be old, but I'm still scrappy," his grandfather returned, while giving him a slight punch in the arm.

Father Mark was not like the priests JP remembered from his childhood. As he had previously noticed, the father was indeed not much older than JP. He seemed as down to earth as anyone he had met. He liked golf and played regularly. In fact, he had even played once or twice with Sam's father, Dr. Atherton.

JP enjoyed breakfast with the two of them and decided then and there that he would need to make this a regular event in his schedule, if it were agreeable to them as well.

After breakfast, JP and his grandfather dropped Father Mark back off at the church and headed back to his grandfather's house.

"Well, what did you think of Father Mark?"

"He's different than what I expected. I mean that in a good way. If it's okay with you, I'd like to come every week, even when classes resume. I really enjoyed this morning."

"That sounds good to me and I'm sure Father Mark would like that. I think he enjoys having someone closer to his age to talk to after Mass."

"Terrific. What's on the agenda for the rest of my stay? Any wild adventures planned?"

"Well, nothing too wild, but I have invited a couple friends over for dinner tonight. I think you'll very much enjoy them."

15

SAM'S BREAK FROM SCHOOL gave her a chance to get back into her music and dancing, which she missed tremendously. It also gave her more time to spend with Captain Jameson.

She had become incredibly fond of him and was impressed by his ascent through the ranks of the Medical Enforcement Unit. At times, the details of his job fascinated her more than what she was learning in medical school. She thought about pursuing a job with the Ministry, like her dad, or perhaps getting into the field of medical enforcement, like the captain. Learning about who should be treated and who shouldn't intrigued her more than treating illness. She was meeting Captain Jameson for dinner at one of the finest restaurants in town. He had been delayed at work so he was unable to pick her up. She entered the restaurant and was surprised to find him already there.

"Hey Sam," the captain said as he stood up and gave her a kiss on the cheek. "Looks like I might have been able to pick you up after all."

"Things go faster at work?"

"Well, it wasn't anything major. I just had to have someone give me an Internal Affairs report."

"Trouble in the ranks?"

"Probably not, but do you remember me telling you about my second-in-command, Lieutenant Osgood? He's the only one on my special team that I didn't handpick. He's been acting a little funny lately and my sources revealed he had a private meeting with your dad."

"Really? Is that unusual?"

"Very unusual. There is a chain of command that should be followed. I've been trying to figure out what he wanted to meet the minister about privately. I don't think he has a beef with me but I guess it's always possible."

"Have you had any conflicts with him recently?"

"I came down a little hard on him a couple months ago when we lost a patient from the End of Life Care Center. It really wasn't his fault, but I was embarrassed by the whole mishap and blew a little steam off in his direction."

"I wouldn't think that would cause him to hold a grudge. Surely he knows that his commanding officer wouldn't take the blame. I'm sure he took it out on someone under him."

"That may be true, but something's up with him ever since the incident at the Care Center. I've actually been having him followed. There's something about that whole affair that doesn't add up, and I trust all the other men on the team implicitly."

"Do you think he found out that he's being followed?"

"I don't think so. My men have been keeping a good distance."

"Maybe it has nothing to do with the Enforcement Unit at all," Sam suggested. "Maybe it's something personal, like marriage problems."

"No way. His marriage is rock solid. He could win Father of the Year from what I hear."

"I could ask Daddy, but more than likely he wouldn't tell me anything. He's always been good at keeping secrets."

"I'm sure he wouldn't have gotten to his powerful position if he hadn't been able to keep secrets."

"He tells me that his job is pretty mundane. Your job, on the other hand, sounds much more exciting. I'd like to learn more about it. Who knows, maybe once I get out of school, I'll get into the enforcement end of medicine. I think as time goes on, more and more diseases are going to be deemed non-treatable. We're being taught in school that people are still expecting to be treated for everything. They don't seem to realize that it costs money and then they complain when taxes are raised."

"Really, Sam, my job isn't as exciting as you might think. Occasionally the raids add a little spice but, for the most part, people seem to respect the law."

"Do you think I could go on a raid with your team? It would definitely add some excitement to all my studying."

"I don't know, Sam. If anything happened to you I might have trouble explaining that to your dad. Anyway, isn't going out with me to this fancy place excitement enough?"

"Of course it is. You never know, it could get more exciting later."

"Oh, I like the sound of that! You're not just trying to butter me up to get your way, are you?"

"Would I do such a thing, *mon Capitan*?" Sam answered with a sly grin on her face.

"Why don't we just order before I break down and say yes?"

"All right, but I won't give up easily," Sam replied coyly.

16

LIEUTENANT OSGOOD WAS TAKING a huge risk in putting the word out that he wanted to make contact with the Underground. Sooner or later, this was likely to get back to Captain Jameson. He would have to come up with some story. Right now, however, the risk really didn't matter to him. Osgood figured that his job was already in jeopardy, but Katie's life was in jeopardy too. Katie's life was all that mattered at the moment.

A meeting with the informant had been arranged over the phone and now Lieutenant Osgood was driving along a circuitous route to the meeting location. This was partly to calm his nerves but also because he again had the feeling he was being tailed. The informant had suggested a bar on the outskirts of town. The lieutenant was vaguely familiar with it from his days as a city cop. It was not a very safe place, even for a cop.

The informant had sounded reliable over the phone and the team had used him before, so Osgood didn't argue with him about the location. The lieutenant knew that he would soon be in more trouble with his own people than he'd be with some degenerates in a bar.

He arrived at the bar about thirty minutes ahead of the sched-uled meet time. Thirty minutes would give him ample time to check the place out. It never hurt to know the avenues of escape should trouble arise. He did a check around the outside of the building, where he noted several windows and only one other exit besides the front door. Several of the windows were covered with steel bars. There were a few cars and a couple of motorcycles parked out in front of the bar.

Following his outside survey, he entered the front door. The inside was fairly dark, especially before his eyes adjusted. It smelled of stale beer, and smoke layered the air like fog rolling across a field at dusk. Once his eyes adjusted, he scanned the room and took note of the various patrons. It was a rough, gritty crowd of mostly bearded and tattooed men playing pool or drinking at the bar. He spotted the door to what looked like a kitchen and deduced that the back door would be through there.

He took a seat at a booth where he could keep an eye on most everyone in the bar as well as an eye on the front door. A waitress came over a couple minutes later, a middle-aged woman who looked as tough as any man in the place. "What can I get ya, honey?" she asked with a Southern drawl.

"I'll have a beer, whatever you have on tap, ma'am." He really had no intention of drinking the beer but figured he better at least play the part. She gave him a long look before heading back to the bar for the beer. It was obvious he didn't fit in at this place.

She returned with the beer and after setting it on the table said, "I ain't never seen you in here before. You here looking for somebody?"

"No, just waiting on a friend."

"Is he a regular?"

"Could be. He suggested we have a drink here."

"What's his name?"

The lieutenant only knew the informant by his first name but feared that if he didn't give a last name it would sound suspicious. "I've always just called him Stevie. I never really asked him his full name."

"You don't mean that sleazy Steve Jones? He's always snooping around here trying to hear information he can sell to the cops. You ain't no cop, are you?"

"No, just an old friend of Stevie's. Actually haven't seen him for a while."

"You better watch your step. Some of these guys in here don't care much for him."

"Thanks. I'll keep that in mind. We're just here to catch up on old times and have a few beers."

She gave the lieutenant a skeptical look and then turned and headed over to the pool table. As she passed the door, a young man with long, wavy hair walked in the front entrance. He was wearing a New York Yankees hat, just as he had said he would on the phone. The waitress evidently recognized him as Stevie and pointed over to the lieutenant's booth. Stevie had a thin build and strutted more than he walked. He had a scraggly beard and looked like he might just live on the same streets where he gathered his information. As he strutted over to the booth, the three guys playing pool stared at him and muttered a few words between them.

"You Osgood?" he asked before he sat down.

"That's me."

"You got my money?"

"You'll see the money when I see the fruits of your labor."

"That wasn't the deal. I told you money up front."

"Well, I'm changing the rules."

"You may be able to do that back at your office but out here, you don't change the rules. You play by my rules. See ya later, asshole," Steve said. He stood up and headed toward the door.

The lieutenant had not expected this, nor had he expected what happened next. As Steve approached the door, the three men playing pool walked over and blocked his exit. Osgood couldn't hear exactly what was being said but it was easy to see things were heating up. He stood up from his booth just as one of the men grabbed Steve around his chest and one of the other men punched him in the stomach. Steve doubled over and would have fallen to the floor, but one man continued to hold him up so his buddy could add a second punch.

Before the second punch was thrown, the lieutenant stepped in. "Do you have a problem with my friend?"

"This scumbag?" the one who had punched him said. "He owes me some money he seems to have forgotten about."

The lieutenant had hoped it wouldn't come to this, but given the circumstances, he had no choice. "Well, unfortunately I can't stand by and let you beat the shit out of my friend."

The three men grinned at each other, but their grins didn't last long. Lieutenant Osgood hit the man who had spoken to him and then kicked the legs out from under the man holding Steve. The man and Steve fell to the floor, with Steve landing on top. The third man had just enough time to grab a pool cue and he struck the lieutenant in the left arm. Osgood was knocked toward a table and chairs but he quickly regained his balance. He grabbed a metal fold-up chair and used it to block the next swing of the pool cue, which snapped in half and went flying across the room. Osgood swung the chair and caught the man across the chest, knocking him to the floor.

With all three of his opponents down, Osgood grabbed Steve by the belt, and lifted him. He dragged him toward the kitchen door as fast as he could. In the kitchen, the lieutenant scanned the room and spotted the rear entrance. He continued dragging

Steve out the back and headed to the car that he had parked there. Steve was still clutching his stomach as Osgood threw him into the passenger seat, just as the three men exited the door. Osgood quickly ran around to the driver's door and got in the car. One of the men swung the broken pool cue and busted out his taillight as Osgood sped away.

Osgood drove for about five minutes until he was sure he had not been followed, and then he pulled over into an empty church parking lot. By then, Steve was looking a little better, but was still holding his stomach.

"Okay, Steve. Now that I saved your ass, we're gonna do it my way and maybe you'll still get paid." Osgood proceeded to explain why he needed to get in contact with the Underground.

Steve paid close attention this time and then replied, "I'll do what I can to arrange an appointment. It might be difficult for anyone to agree to even consider it though, given your position."

"Just remember, Steve, I know how to find you and the next time I won't be so anxious to help you. In fact, I might just take you back to that bar myself."

Steve nodded in understanding as the lieutenant dropped him off back downtown.

17

JP WASN'T SURE WHAT to expect from his grandfather, who was always full of surprises. But then again, that's what made him so fun to be around. He had left to pick up the two mystery guests for dinner. He had prepared the entire dinner himself, although he had left JP in charge of taking the cake out of the oven at the right time. JP wanted to make sure it was done correctly, as it was his only assignment. JP sat down in the living room and put on some music. His thoughts drifted back to the Mass earlier in the day. He had been raised in the faith but it had not played a big part in his parents' lives. They had gone through the motions for many years, going to Mass on Sundays and taking JP with them. They eventually started going only intermittently and then not at all. As with many of their generation, the secular world became their place of worship, which made passage of the Medical Reconciliation Act that much easier.

JP had fallen in line with his parents and until this morning had given little thought about organized religion. He had always believed in a higher power and the reality of evil. However, in church earlier in the day, he seemed to have found a clearer understanding of good and evil. He had felt a definite power inside those four walls.

He heard the garage door open, indicating his grandfather's return, and he walked back into the kitchen to welcome the guests as they came through the back door from the garage.

When the first person came in, what he saw shocked him.

"Hi. I'm Willy. What's your name?"

JP stood staring for some time before his grandfather walked in and said, "Aren't you going to introduce yourself?"

JP regained his composure and said, "Hi. I'm JP. Nice to meet you, Willy."

Willy walked past JP and said, "Smells good. What's for dinner?"

JP turned around and again stared at Willy. He had never seen a Down's syndrome adult before and had trouble keeping his eyes off him. However, when the next guest came in, it was easy for him to remove his eyes from Willy. The cute girl with blond hair he had seen in church stepped into the kitchen. She stuck her hand out and said, "Hi, JP. I'm Emily Johns. Your grandfather has told me a lot about you."

JP knew his grandfather was full of surprises, but these two guests had JP floored.

"Very nice to meet you, Emily. I think I saw you in church this morning, didn't I?"

"Yes. I've been attending St. Francis for a while now."

"So my grandfather has told me. Have we met before? You look familiar but I can't seem to place you."

"Yes and no. I think it would be better for your grandfather to explain."

JP incredulously looked over at his grandfather who waved him off and said, "Later, JP. Right now I think Willy's hungry and dinner shouldn't be kept waiting."

"Okay. But I think you have quite a bit of explaining to do."

Dinner was as delicious as expected, but JP had a hard time taking his eyes off the two guests. He had seen pictures of Down's adults in textbooks, but here was one right in front of him. He was not what JP had expected from what he'd seen in the books. Willy was a jovial, friendly man who was absolutely charming. There was no pretense in him at all. He engaged in excellent conversation, especially when it came to golf.

Emily was obviously very educated—and beautiful—a nice combination in any young man's mind. JP noticed, however, that she tended to repeat some mannerisms, such as sitting her silverware down on the table in a precisely parallel fashion.

Following dinner, Emily and JP's grandfather carried the dishes back to the kitchen, leaving JP alone with Willy. It took no time for Willy to start talking. "Are you a doctor like Dr. John?"

"Not yet, Willy. I'm in school to become a doctor."

"Will you help Dr. John do his work?"

"Grandpa doesn't work anymore. He used to be a doctor."

"He still works at my house. He's a very good doctor."

"What do you mean he still works at your house, Willy?"

"When new people come to our house at the church, Dr. John checks them."

"What people come to your house, Willy?"

"New people. Don't know where they come from."

"Does Emily live at your house?"

"Yes. She's nice to Willy. I like her. She's pretty, too."

"She sure is, Willy. Did Grandpa, I mean Dr. John, have to check her when she came to your house?"

"Yes. She was sick when she came to the house."

"When did she come to your house, Willy?"

"Not sure. Not good with time."

JP was becoming more confused by the minute. His grandfather had some explaining to do for sure.

JP and Willy were still chatting as JP's grandfather and Emily returned from doing the dishes. His grandfather had the smile of a Cheshire cat as he entered the living room.

"Have you and Willy been having a good conversation, JP?"

"Oh, yeah. He's been telling me all about you and your practice over at his house."

His grandfather replied with a good chuckle. "Oh he has, has he? Well, he's always one for a good story."

"So you're telling me you're not still practicing medicine?"

"Well, I didn't say that, exactly."

Emily sat across from JP watching his expressions as the conversation progressed. She found him not only attractive but she also felt a warmth from him. She had a feeling this evening was going to be important, not only for the Medical Underground, but also for her personally. At least she hoped so.

"Okay, Grandpa, perhaps it's time you tell me what's going on here."

"Are you sure you really want to know? It will not only change your future but could put you at some risk."

"Well, I figured that the moment Willy walked in tonight. I think I'm up to it."

"Okay. I'm sure by now you and your classmates have heard rumors of a so-called Medical Underground. They raid pharmacies and rescue and treat patients headed for the End of Life Care Centers. Well, you're looking at two examples, which prove those rumors are more than just rumors."

JP listened intently as his grandfather continued. "Willy here was actually the first person rescued locally, following the institution of the Medical Reconciliation Act. Unfortunately, as you probably know, most Down's adults and children were not so lucky. He has lived in various safe houses for almost thirty years and has been a great help to the Underground. He's a legend in our circles."

JP looked over at Willy, who had a huge but bashful smile on his face. When JP glanced over at Emily, his grandfather took the cue.

"Emily was rescued just two to three months ago. In fact, a young man gave his life rescuing her."

JP noticed Emily dropped her eyes down, almost as if in prayer. He wondered what it must feel like to know someone had died so that you might live. He felt instant empathy for her.

"Emily has given me permission to tell you the rest of her story. Emily is a bright, young engineer, who unfortunately has OCD. She was working on her master's degree when others began to notice some of her ritualistic mannerisms. She was essentially forced to undergo an evaluation and once the diagnosis was made, she was scheduled for the End of Life Care Center."

"Wait a minute. This is sounding all too familiar. When did you say this all happened?"

"It was about two to three months ago, JP."

JP had a flash of recognition and he gasped. "Now I remember. Her case was presented in one of our classes. Now I know why Emily looked familiar to me in church earlier." He studied her features. "She looks different now."

Emily lifted her head up and said, "It's the hair. My natural hair color is dark. Once I recovered following the rescue, it was recommended that I change my name and my hair color. It's a small price to pay to avoid a return trip to the morgue."

"The morgue?" JP queried.

Emily's lush lips tightened for a moment. "The so-called End of Life Care Center."

Dr. Patrick continued with Emily's story. "Once she was rescued, we began treatment for her OCD while she stayed at the safe house. She has responded well to medication and could now probably get by in public without anyone noticing that she has OCD. As they may have told you in class, it's unlikely that she will be totally cured. However, what they may not have told you is that with treatment, many patients with OCD can function very well in society and lead very productive lives."

JP was having trouble taking it all in. "Does Emily have to stay in hiding for the rest of her life?"

"That's always the million-dollar question. Some of our rescued people have been treated and given new identities. Unfortunately even with the new identities, we can't change their DNA. If they are ever seen again by the government-run healthcare system, their record will come up with a red flag and they might be right back where they were before they were rescued. Obviously, some like Willy here have to stay hidden forever."

"Has Emily gotten a new identity yet?"

"We're working on that. She's too young and bright to keep hidden away forever."

JP got a little grin on his face and he said, "I was wondering if she would be safe going out to dinner with me sometime?"

Dr. Patrick smiled and looked over at Emily whose face was now turning several shades of red. "I think that would be entirely up to Emily. Provided she doesn't have a run-in with the law or need any medical care, she should be totally safe. It's very unlikely that anyone would recognize her even if she hadn't dyed her hair."

"How about it, Emily?"

Emily looked over at Dr. Patrick. The older man didn't respond so she looked back at JP and said, "I'd love to, but maybe just not yet. I think I need a little more time to adjust to this new life. This is actually about the farthest I've ventured away from St. Francis since I was rescued."

"Well, I'll definitely take a rain check."

JP's grandpa was thoroughly enjoying this scene. From the first time he had talked to Emily when she came out of her sedated state, he knew she was a beautiful person inside and out. She was a perfect match for his kindhearted grandson.

"Okay, JP, now that my little secret life is out on the table, we need to a have a serious talk. This is truly a life-and-death operation, not only for the patients we help but also for those involved in the organization. As I mentioned earlier, a young man died rescuing Emily. I need to tell you that what we do is highly illegal. If we are caught helping, harboring, or treating any of these patients, we could be facing imprisonment or even a trip to the End of Life Care Center ourselves. Also, the organization is much larger than just me and a few other people. I don't call the shots. We don't make the decisions on who gets saved or which pharmacies are raided. We have to be willing to take orders."

As if thinking aloud, JP asked, "Who is in charge of the organization?"

"I don't actually know for sure and couldn't divulge it anyway if I did. The fewer who know the hierarchy of the organization, the better. Beyond this region, I don't even know if any true organization exists."

"This is all well and good and I can understand why you're doing this, but why are you telling me about it?"

His grandfather paused a moment, looked over at Emily.

"Well JP, I'm not getting any younger so we are always looking for new recruits for the cause. During our conversations over the last few months, I got the impression you were of the same mind as me with regard to the Act. After some thought and consultation with others, it was decided to ask you to join our group."

"What would this mean in terms of my medical school training?"

"Nothing at all at the present. You would continue in school as usual. There could be times where you might be asked to do some minor things, but for the time being you're more valuable to us in getting as much training as you can. Once you're out of training, your role would become more active. You would need to learn treatment protocols that are not being taught to you in school now because they're no longer approved by the government. You see, JP, that's part of the reason I've been so useful to them. I'm old enough and still knowledgeable enough in the way things used to be that I can treat people with methods not available today. I'm also kept busy passing on my knowledge, so we will have a steady stream of physicians who can continue once I'm not able to practice."

"What if I don't think I'm up to it?"

"It's up to you, JP. Whatever you decide, we obviously depend on you to keep our involvement secret."

"That goes without saying, Grandpa. I'm just not sure I'm up to all this cloak and dagger stuff."

"Well, you don't have to decide right now. I can only say it's given me more reward than all of my other adventures put together."

JP looked deep into his grandfather's eyes. There was no mistaking that he meant what he said.

"I'll keep that in mind."

18

LIEUTENANT OSGOOD HAD MADE it clear to Steve what he needed for his little daughter. A few days went by before he heard back from him. The delay didn't make him too happy. He still didn't know how much time he had before Katie would be summoned to the End of Life Care Center.

Finally, Steve contacted him and said that a meeting had been arranged for him with someone involved in the Underground. Osgood was quite nervous about this meeting for numerous reasons, not the least of which was his position with the MEU. He wondered how anyone in the Underground could possibly trust him. They had to be wondering if this was a trap.

To add to his fears, he believed someone had been following him. If it was the captain and he found out that Osgood was dealing with the Underground, Osgood's career was over. More importantly, he could lose his family.

He had been instructed to come alone and was given another circuitous route to his destination. He had been given a phone number to call for the final directions once he arrived. After placing the call, he was instructed to walk a block and enter a men's clothing store. Inside the store, he was to pick out a pair of pants and enter the dressing room.

Inside the dressing room, he was met by a young man. "Are you Osgood?"

"Yes, I am. Who are you?"

"No one of importance. I'm not even sure who you are meeting or why. I was just paid to come in here and make sure you were not wearing any kind of tracking or monitoring devices."

"So you have no idea of who I am or what I am looking for?"

"I have no idea, nor do I want to know. I am just hired to do one task and that's the way I like it."

"Okay, then. Let's get this over with."

"Okay. Please remove your clothes including your underwear."

"You've got to be kidding."

"No, sir. I am just doing as I was instructed."

The lieutenant reluctantly removed all of his clothes as instructed and then was told to remove his watch as well. The young man examined the clothes carefully to make sure nothing was sewn into them. He then gave the lieutenant back his clothes and told him to get dressed though he kept the watch. He said it would be returned to Osgood later.

Osgood was not pleased about leaving his watch and he figured he would never see it again. He handed it over and the young man reached into his pocket. Swiftly, Osgood grabbed his wrist and put a tight hold on him.

Obviously taken aback by the lieutenant's aggression, the young man said, "Whoa, man. I just have to give you an envelope."

Reluctantly, the lieutenant let loose and stepped back. "Sorry, I'm just a little on edge about all this."

The young man handed him the envelope, turned, and quickly exited the dressing room. Osgood opened the envelope and read his final instructions. He left the new pair of pants in the dressing room, departed the store, and headed to what he hoped was finally the meeting location.

The young man stood behind a rack of clothes and watched as the lieutenant exited the dressing room and then the store. He quickly followed him from a distance, to complete his final task. He had to make sure the lieutenant placed no calls and didn't speak to anyone on the way to his meeting with the doctor. If he saw Osgood do either, the meeting would be aborted.

※ ※ ※

Dr. Patrick was nervous about his upcoming meeting. Since starting his work with the Underground, he had helped people from just about all walks of life, including politicians, judges, and even other doctors. They all had been trying to avoid the End of Life Care Center or were trying to go around the system to get treatment that was otherwise unavailable. However, Dr. Patrick had never had to deal with someone from the Medical Enforcement Unit, let alone the second-in-command. Yet he had received orders to meet with Lieutenant Osgood today. This smelled like a trap to him, but the recommendation to follow through with the meeting had come from the highest ranks of the organization. Dr. Patrick waited for the MEU lieutenant in a small restaurant, sitting in a corner well away from any of the other patrons. Although he was nervous, his curiosity gave him a sense of adventure and a calmness that he didn't expect, and the more he thought about it, the more he relaxed. Hopefully, time wouldn't prove him wrong.

Osgood entered the restaurant and, once his eyes adjusted to the dim light, he scanned the room for any potential problems, noticing an older-looking man sitting at a corner table by himself.

The man was wearing a beige-colored tam as had been described in the directions that Osgood had gotten from the young man. Osgood walked toward the table. He thought the man might be yet another messenger he'd have to deal with before getting to someone that could actually help him. However, as he got closer to the table, he noticed that this elderly man looked more-fit than he had expected. Perhaps he was a more important player after all.

"I'm Osgood."

"Please be seated. I understand you have a particular need."

"Before I waste my time, I need to know if you're someone that can actually help or just another messenger boy."

"That remains to be seen," Dr. Patrick replied. "You talk to me or no one else."

The lieutenant looked around the restaurant one more time and then sat down and got to the point. "All right then. I'm sure you are probably aware of who I am but I'm here as a father, a father of a sick little girl who happens to mean everything to me." The lieutenant paused because he was still having trouble coping with the situation.

Dr. Patrick could tell the lieutenant was sincere. "Go on. I'm listening."

Osgood's voice shook as he continued. "My wife and I recently found out that Katie, my five-year-old daughter, has leukemia, a form not treatable, according to her pediatrician. Or should I say, a form the government does not allow them to treat. From what we found out, Katie's form of the disease used to have about a forty to fifty percent cure rate, with appropriate chemotherapy. Unfortunately, that rate is not good enough according to the Act and she is going to be scheduled for the End of Life Care Center. I can't let that happen. She is my only daughter."

"What makes you think that we can help you?"

"I don't know. I'm obviously aware of what the Underground

does and I am out of other options."

Dr. Patrick looked the lieutenant straight in the eyes for a few moments. "Where is Katie right now? Has she been admitted to the hospital?"

"No, she is still at home with us. She is actually not feeling sick at all right now. The leukemia was found on a routine preschool physical."

As the lieutenant looked on with pleading eyes, Dr. Patrick pondered the situation for a moment.

He didn't want to raise the lieutenant's hopes. He also knew that getting Katie appropriately treated would be extremely dangerous. It would take significant planning as well as a lot of luck. He was not sure he had the resources to pull it off. Then again, for a five-year-old little girl, how could he not make the effort?

"I want you to understand that it will be difficult to accomplish what you ask. You must be aware that the risks are significant for us as well as for you and your family."

"My wife is unaware of this meeting, but I am obviously well aware of the risks and willing to take the chance."

"You must also realize that if she is successfully treated, she will most likely have to be placed with another family, to avoid future detection."

Osgood was clearly shocked. He had not considered that possibility, but, as he thought about it, he realized there would be no other choice. It would be difficult for him and his wife, but at least Katie would be alive. "That hadn't occurred to me, but if that's what it takes to keep her alive, then so be it."

"One last question. In your position, do you think there will be any way you can assist us in procuring the needed medications for her treatment?"

The lieutenant had expected this question but was unsure of the answer. "I'm sure you know if anyone finds out about this, my career is over and I could go to prison. I can't be sure that I can help. All I can say is I will try if I have the opportunity."

"That's fair enough, but we will use your position if necessary."

"What do we do now?" the lieutenant asked.

"You walk out of here and do nothing out of the ordinary until we contact you."

"I want you to know we greatly appreciate the risks you are taking for our daughter. I will not forget it."

The lieutenant stood, shook Dr. Patrick's hand. As he left, he noticed the young man from the clothing store standing across the street. He figured the young man's task was finished for now and that he would never see his watch again.

19

WHEN SCHOOL RESUMED, JP had trouble getting his mind off of all that had transpired at his grandfather's house. The more he thought about working with the Underground someday, the more it appealed to him. Doctors were never meant to make the kind of decisions being forced upon them by the Medical Reconciliation Act. JP knew that now more than ever after meeting Willy and Emily. To think that someone as beautiful, intelligent, and vibrant as Emily had been minutes away from termination gave him cold chills. He just couldn't see himself sending someone like that or anyone, for that matter, to the End of Life Care Center.

As his thoughts drifted back to Emily, he wondered if she would indeed give him a rain check for a date. Other than Sam, she was the first woman to really catch his eye and he definitely planned to pursue a relationship with her. He was still somewhat daydreaming about her when Sam walked up to him and brought him back to reality.

"Can you believe we're finally getting out of the classroom and into the hospital to see real patients? It seems like all that basic science took forever."

"I know what you mean. I'm anxious to move on too."

Sam seemed to have an air of excitement about her that he hadn't noticed before. He wondered if it was truly about getting out of the classroom or about her new relationship.

"You still seeing that guy you introduced me to before break?"

"Yes. We spent quite a bit of time together over the holiday."

"He seems nice enough. What does he do?"

"He's in charge of the MEU for this region. He reports directly to Daddy. Daddy introduced us at a dinner a few months ago."

"Oh, really. I guess I'd better watch what I say around you now," JP said with a little chuckle.

"Oh, yeah. Like you'd have something to worry about, JP," she responded with a smile on her face.

JP changed the subject. "Have you done your first history and physical on a patient in the hospital yet?"

"No, not yet. I'm heading over now. How about you?"

"I just finished it. It felt funny putting on a white coat for the first time and seeing a real patient. I had a nice elderly man who was pretty healthy overall. He was admitted for anemia. I think he probably just has an ulcer so hopefully he'll be able to get treatment. I hope he doesn't end up having something we can't treat. I'd hate to see him get a one-way ticket to the End of Life Care Center. He really seemed nice and has a bunch of grandchildren."

"Isn't it amazing that we'll soon be making those decisions ourselves?"

"I don't know, Sam. I'm not so sure any human being should have the right to make those decisions for another person. My grandfather told me that a long time ago, doctors used to be treated like gods in the hospital. Now it's almost like we are playing God with other people's lives. It just doesn't seem right."

"Oh, come on, JP. You're starting to sound like some religious fanatic. What happened to the old JP who was so gung-ho to be a doctor? Did you have a *Road to Damascus* experience over the break?"

JP was caught off guard by Sam's question and visibly tightened up. There was no way he was going to tell her about Emily and Willy, especially after finding out who the guy was that she was dating. In addition, he was also surprised that Sam even knew the Bible story of St. Paul and his encounter with Jesus on the road to Damascus. He was pretty sure she was irreligious and an agnostic.

"No. Nothing special happened over break. I'm just saying that it seems like we could treat more people than we do, rather than just send them off to be terminated. Aren't we devaluing life when we do that?"

"That might be true, JP, but remember what the professor was saying last semester about how the money we save treating these questionable cases allows more people to be treated in the long run. Don't you believe that, JP?"

"I know there's some truth to that but it seems like there should be a better way. That's all I'm saying."

"Whatever, JP. I see nothing wrong with the way things are now, and lately I have a better appreciation for the importance of Daddy's job. In fact, I wouldn't mind following in his footsteps. You should talk to him. It sounds like you need to get your head on straight if you're going to stay in medical school."

JP couldn't believe this was the same Sam that he had an attraction to at one time. They seemed worlds apart. The last thing he needed to do now was talk to her dad. He realized he needed to be careful about what he said to Sam, now more than ever.

"Sam, you know me. I'm cool with the system. I just like to mix things up once in a while."

"Well, stop it. You scare me when you talk like that. I need my study-buddy around for a few more years."

"Oh, you'd do just fine on your own. After all, it seems like you've found someone else to spend your time with."

"You know what I mean, JP. Sure I'm spending a lot of time with Mike, but you're still my med school buddy. I'd be lost without you."

"Well, that's nice to hear, Sam. I do miss our studying together in the library."

"Okay, then. I'm glad that's settled. More time in the library coming up. Listen, I gotta run to my history and physical. Really, if you want to talk to Daddy sometime, I can arrange it. Just say the word."

"Thanks for the offer, Sam. I'll be just fine. I'll see you later."

As Sam walked away, JP again thought that her dad was the last person he would want to talk to and that the Ministry of Health was the last place he would want to go.

20

DR. PATRICK HOPED THAT exposing JP to the Underground wasn't a mistake. He had no doubt that JP's heart was pure and that he supported the Underground's mission, but he might not be prepared for all that was involved. It may have been better to wait until he graduated—but what was done was done. Hopefully, he could keep JP uninvolved until that time.

Dr. Patrick had more urgent matters on his mind. He had to devise a plan to abduct the daughter of the second-in-command of the Enforcement Unit and get her treated. He had executed many missions since getting involved with the Underground, but this one worried him more than any other, because of the girl's complicated health issues and her father's treacherous employment situation.

If Dr. Patrick could pull this off, he knew that Lieutenant Osgood would be eternally grateful, which might prove useful to the Underground in the future.

Along with two of his friends who had helped him on a few other missions, Thomas arrived on time at Dr. Patrick's house.

The first of these friends, Matthew, was a very quiet young man, but his appearance spoke volumes. He was six foot four and appeared to be made of pure muscle. His demeanor did not match his appearance. He was soft-spoken and gentle, always the first to offer a helping hand to anyone in need.

Thomas's other friend, Samuel, was slim, if not downright scrawny, and extremely outgoing. He talked to anyone and everyone. He did enough talking for both himself and Matthew most of the time.

"Good evening, everyone. Come on into the living room. We're still waiting for Father Mark and Emily."

"It'll be good to see Emily again," Thomas replied. It's hard to believe it's been almost three months since William was shot rescuing her. I'm still having a hard time getting over that. I'm sure seeing her doing well will help."

"I'm sure it will," Dr. Patrick replied. "Can I get anyone anything to eat or drink while we wait?"

Matthew's eyes lit up at that and he said, "Do you have any of those chocolate chip cookies we had the last time we were here?"

"I made a special batch just for you, Matthew," Dr. Patrick said as he headed to the kitchen. "Anything to drink, anyone?"

※ ※ ※

Emily was nervous about the meeting at Dr. Patrick's house. Her OCD had markedly improved since starting her medication following her rescue, but meeting new people always seemed to bring out some of her rituals. Sooner or later though, she had to come out of hiding in the safe house and try to reestablish a new life for herself.

She couldn't believe how things had changed in just three short months. She had lost a lot, but knew there was no going back to her old life. And in many ways, she didn't want to. Although she had done well in school and been looking forward to a career in engineering, her OCD had dominated her life. There was not a waking moment that she hadn't gotten various obsessive thoughts, which would lead to the rituals that would undo the bad thoughts. She had done a good job of hiding it from everyone since its onset when she was thirteen, but as time went on, the rituals had become more frequent and overt. She had thought she was crazy and was quite embarrassed by it. She also had thought she was the only one who had ever had the disorder. Therefore, she had never even considered seeking help.

All that had changed now. She didn't like taking the medication, but she felt better than she had in years. The obsessions weren't gone, but they had diminished, as had the anxiety they produced. Her biggest regret was that William had died saving her. Her OCD had caused her to be very self-centered and had consumed her every waking moment. She couldn't change that, but she could build on her current situation by rescuing and helping others through the Underground. She went upstairs into the church, knelt down before the tabernacle, and prayed. She knew it was going to take more strength than she had to carry out her new life.

While she was praying, Father Mark walked in.

"Are you ready to head over to Dr. Patrick's?"

"I think so, Father. I have to get on with my life at some point and I think it's time to give back for what's been given to me."

"I couldn't agree with you more, but we all want to make sure you're ready."

"I'll be okay. After all, I've got your boss on my side," she replied with a smile on her face.

As Emily and Father Mark drove to Dr. Patrick's house, Emily wondered if JP would be at the meeting. He had seemed like a really nice young man and hadn't appeared to be turned off by her problem. Instead he had actually asked her out on a date. She had tried dating only once since her OCD had started and it had been a disaster. The young man she had gone out with had noticed some of her rituals, and when he asked her about them, she initially denied that anything was wrong at all. However, when he questioned her about it again, she opened up to him about her problem. At first he seemed sympathetic, but after that evening, he never called or spoke to her again. She had decided then and there if she ever did date again, she would not divulge her secret to anyone. JP knew about her OCD so she didn't need to worry about telling him or not telling him.

They arrived at Dr. Patrick's house and went in. Emily was disappointed when she saw that JP was not present. She and Father Mark were introduced to Thomas, Matthew, and Samuel, and then Dr. Patrick got down to the matter at hand.

21

LIEUTENANT OSGOOD WAS WAITING for Captain Jameson at the Ministry of Health. He was unsure what the captain
wanted but figured that being summoned was not good. Nothing
had happened with Katie since Osgood's meeting with the Underground agent and he was getting nervous. He knew the call from
the End of Life Care Center would come soon, but there wasn't
much else he could do but wait.

The captain showed up and motioned for the lieutenant to
follow him into the office. He looked very serious and there was
no friendly bantering. Osgood followed him into the office and
stood until Captain Jameson asked him to have a seat.

"Jaye, I'm sure you're aware that you are the only member
of my team I didn't personally handpick. That aside, your resume is stellar and the Minister of Health stands behind you one
hundred percent. However, over the past few months, I've had
some concern about your performance. In addition, it has come
to my attention that recently you seem to be distracted. Is there
anything going on that I should know?"

The lieutenant quickly pondered his current situation. He and his wife had told no one about Katie's health problems except for the Minister of Health. And no one, not even his wife, knew that he made contact with the Underground—at least, he didn't think so. But the captain's comments again made the lieutenant wonder if he wasn't being followed. If he was, more than likely the captain already knew about the lieutenant's activities.

"No, sir. There's nothing going on other than the usual chaos when you have five kids running around the house," he said with a laugh, trying to sound as relaxed as possible. "I guess I'm surprised that people are concerned about my work. I was under the impression that the unit has had an excellent record since you came on board, Captain."

"That is true, Jaye, but the more I think about the incident at the End of Life Care Center a few months ago, the more I think the Underground has access to our activities."

"That's interesting that you bring that up, sir, because I've been wondering the same thing." The lieutenant now relaxed a little, knowing that the captain was more concerned about an incident several months ago than with his own recent activities trying to secure help for Katie.

✳ ✳ ✳

The lieutenant's wife was across town, waiting to pick up her boys from school. Katie was seated in the back seat of the minivan, excitedly awaiting her brothers. Janet Osgood was a loving mother and devoted wife. Her life revolved around her family. She had come from a dysfunctional background and had made a vow never to allow anything to come before family. She had been lucky enough to meet Jaye, who also had a strong commitment to family, probably more so than she did. He, unlike her, had come from a very loving family. It was two different backgrounds but one philosophy—family above all.

Janet had been a nervous wreck since Katie had been diagnosed. She'd had nightmares every night about Katie being taken to the End of Life Care Center. She was exhausted. Though she was trying to keep herself together for the sake of Jaye and the children, she didn't know how long she could carry the burden.

Jaye's behavior wasn't helping her either. Since Katie had been diagnosed, Jaye had been very quiet. She had tried to get him to talk about Katie, but he'd avoided the issue. In addition, he had left the house on several occasions without telling her where he was going, which was not like him at all.

She was on the verge of crying when she heard the school's bell ring. Wiping tears, she started looking for the boys, who would be coming out different doors. She had to keep herself together.

※ ※ ※

Thomas, Matthew, Samuel, and Emily were preparing for the mission at Dr. Patrick's house. Everybody seemed relatively calm, except Emily. This would be her debut. Although she was nervous, she was also excited about finally being able to start helping the Underground.

Dr. Patrick briefed them once again about the goal of the mission. For the most part, it was quite straightforward. They were going to abduct a little girl who was destined for the End of Life Care Center. He had initially thought about not telling them who she was, but then decided it was their right to know who they were saving.

"Are you kidding me?!" Thomas said, incredulous.

"No, I'm not. He approached us and I was told that his story is legitimate. It makes me nervous too, but he does seem desperate."

"Sounds like a trap to me," Thomas retorted. "Why should we help the man whose job it is to enforce the very thing we're against? Why shouldn't he have to sleep in the bed he's helped make?"

"Your point is well taken. However, we'll be helping an innocent little girl more than him. I know it doesn't seem kosher but we have our instructions. If anyone wants to bow out, I'll understand. There's no question this mission has higher-than-normal risks, but I for one can't tolerate the idea that a five-year-old little girl, who could possibly be cured, is going to be terminated."

One by one, they looked at each other and they all agreed to proceed, although Thomas was the last.

"Okay, then. The only other thing of which I want you to be aware is that we're not sure if the lieutenant's wife knows that the child is going to be abducted. Realize that she will most likely resist and will most likely get hysterical. We will rendezvous back at St. Francis at the safe house."

※ ※ ※

The lieutenant was still sitting in the captain's office discussing the incident at the End of Life Care Center.

"Jaye, do you have any idea where we could have a leak?"

"No, sir. I've been giving it some thought but haven't come up with any concrete ideas. You obviously know these guys better than I do, but I can't see any of them betraying the unit."

"I agree. There has to be some explanation. There's just no way that that incident could have succeeded without inside information."

"I've also come to that same conclusion, sir. I will keep looking into it."

Captain Jameson was feeling a little better about Lieutenant

Osgood but still harbored reservations. He would continue the intermittent surveillance. "Is there anything I can do to ease things at home? Being single, I guess I can't appreciate the stresses of having a family."

The lieutenant stiffened at the mention of his family, but the captain seemed genuinely concerned for his welfare.

"No it's just the usual everyday trials and tribulations of having kids. It has its ups and downs, for sure."

✵ ✵ ✵

Mrs. Osgood picked up her boys from school and headed home. She had one quick stop to make on the way. She hoped Jaye would be home when they arrived, but doubted it. She could use a break from the kids to get a little rest. She planned to stop to pick up a pizza for dinner. She normally cooked dinner every night so the family could all spend time around the table hearing about each other's day, while they ate. Having dinner together helped form a cohesive bond for the family. But tonight, she didn't think she had the energy or the will power. Distracted and fatigued, Mrs. Osgood didn't notice the unmarked van that had been following her since she left the school.

✵ ✵ ✵

Thomas and his associates had watched as Mrs. Osgood waited for her boys at the school. They considered taking their subject at that time; however, there had been too many other parents waiting for their children. They followed her at a distance, under the assumption she would be heading home with all the kids. They planned to wait till she parked at home and then would snatch the little girl. Their only concern was whether her husband would be home at the time. Lieutenant Osgood was not told when—or if—the Underground would act. If he was present during the abduction he'd have to try and stop the kidnappers or risk being charged as an accomplice. Janet Osgood arrived at the pizzeria and pulled into a parking place. The store was at the end of a large shopping mall and readily accessible. As her mother was exiting the car, Katie asked if she could go in with her. The boys showed no interest and were discussing plans for fishing with their father during the upcoming weekend.

As Janet and Katie entered the pizzeria, a white van pulled into a parking space a few spots away. Just like before, Janet was paying little attention to her surroundings. Inside the store, she placed her order as Katie skipped around looking at various pictures on the walls.

Janet watched her little girl and again wondered if the pediatrician had been wrong. Katie looked too healthy to have a deadly disease. Perhaps they should ask the doctor to repeat the tests. Maybe the results had been misinterpreted. Maybe Katie was as healthy as any other little girl. Perhaps this nightmare was nothing more than a mistake. More than likely, a repeat of the test would be out of the question, especially after Jaye's violent outburst in the pediatrician's office. She would have to talk to Jaye about this—if she could get him to talk about it all.

Outside the pizza place, Thomas and the rest of his team watched as their subject entered the store. Thomas quietly discussed with the others whether they should go ahead and grab the little girl here, rather than wait until the family arrived at home. It was more public here, but at least they wouldn't have to worry about the woman's husband being home.

Every now and then, Janet walked to the door of the pizza parlor and looked out to check on the boys. They seemed to be fine in the car and were engaged in conversation. She and Jaye had not informed the boys of Katie's situation. They really didn't know how to tell them. She knew the brothers loved their little sister and would be devastated when they were told.

Janet paid for the pizza and she and Katie exited the store. Katie wanted to carry the pizza so she could show her brothers that she was helping make dinner.

Thomas backed the van out of the parking space. Matthew was riding in the passenger's seat and Emily and Samuel were in the back, adjacent to the sliding doors of the van. As the little girl and her mother approached their minivan, Thomas pulled his van behind it and blocked its exit. Matthew and Emily quickly jumped out.

Janet was walking behind Katie. Her mind was busy thinking about everything but her surroundings. She hardly noticed the van that had pulled behind her car or the large man and petite young woman quickly stepping toward her.

The large man took the pizzas from Katie and laid them on the sidewalk while the young woman grabbed Katie and headed to the minivan.

"What are you doing?" GIVE ME MY DAUGHTER!" Janet screamed as she lurched toward the woman whisking away Katie.

Janet was quickly restrained by the large man who had taken the pizzas. Joshua, Katie's thirteen-year-old oldest brother, jumped out of the minivan and tried to go after his sister. He too was gently restrained by the large man as the young woman closed the sliding side door of their van.

An off-duty security guard heading to his car heard the scream. He saw the hysterical woman and a little girl being carried toward an unmarked van. He ran toward the lady and, as he did, he pulled a small handgun from the small of his back. He was not licensed to carry a gun and had strict orders never to bring one to work.

Emily loaded the little girl into the van. Out of the corner of his eye, Matthew noticed a uniformed young man running in their direction. He turned and looked at the man directly and saw that he was aiming a pistol in his direction. "Emily, get in the van now!" Matthew yelled.

Emily jumped into the van with the girl just as Matthew let go of the lady and little boy. He lurched toward the van, trying to dive in the opened sliding door. Just as he reached it, he heard a shot and then the lady screamed again. Matthew turned and saw the young boy he had restrained lying on the ground. He was crying and holding his stomach. A pool of blood was forming on the pavement under him.

Matthew ran back to the little boy and bent down to check him just as the man holding the gun came up to the scene. The boy was bleeding, but alert.

Matthew turned and confronted the uniformed man. "You stupid idiot! You shot this little boy."

"I—I—I was just trying to stop you from taking that little girl."

"You didn't even know what was going on."

The security guard dropped the small pistol, turned, and ran toward his car. Matthew started to go after him and then heard sirens in the distance. He turned around, scooped up Joshua, and raced to the van. As he ran he looked back at Janet Osgood and shouted, "We'll do everything we can for both of them." He leapt into the van with Joshua as Janet stood staring at the bloody spot on the pavement. It was probably a minute before Mark, her next oldest boy, was able to get her attention.

"Mom! Mom!" he was screaming. "Call Dad! He'll know what to do!"

Slowly, she looked at Mark and mumbled, "What?"

"You've got to call Dad *now,*" he repeated, as the sirens drew near.

※ ※ ※

Lieutenant Osgood was still in Captain Jameson's office when his cell phone rang.

"Honey! Slow down. You're not making any sense."

"Katie and Joshua, gone. They're gone. Joshua shot. Bleeding bad."

"Honey, slow down. Tell me where you are?" Through the phone, the lieutenant heard sirens in the background.

Janet slowly began making sense and told her husband what had happened. The lieutenant instantly realized that the Underground must have set their plan in motion for trying to save Katie, but he couldn't get a grip on how Joshua was involved. "Janet! What exactly happened to Joshua and where is he now?"

"As two people were kidnapping Katie, Joshua jumped out of our van and tried to help. Then some man in a uniform came running up and the next thing I know, he shot a pistol. The man who shot the gun then dropped it and ran. The big man picked up Joshua and said they would do everything they could for the both of them."

"Okay. Just stay there. Don't say anything to the police until I get there."

The lieutenant hung up his cell phone and stood to leave.

"What's going on?" the captain asked.

"It's my kids. Two of them have been abducted and one of them was shot by what sounds like a cop or security guard. My wife is hysterical. I have to go, sir."

※ ※ ※

Thomas drove as fast as he could without drawing attention. The little girl was crying hysterically and the young boy was moaning in pain. Emily was doing what she could to calm the little girl down but was not having much luck.

"Matthew, what happened out there and why did you bring the boy?" Thomas questioned.

"When I saw that young boy bleeding, I just thought we had to do something to help him."

"It might have been better to leave him there so he could have been taken to the hospital. I'm not sure Dr. Patrick is equipped to take care of a gunshot to the stomach."

"I know. It was just a gut response. I better call the doctor and let him know we have an additional guest—one who probably needs surgery."

22

DR. PATRICK PACED THE floor at his home, waiting for a call from his team. He was worried about how Emily would do on her first mission but knew in his heart it had been good to get her involved.

He planned to meet his team at the St. Francis safe house once they were on their way after picking up the little girl. The first task would be to get her to relax and trust them. He hoped Emily would be of great help in that regard. He had arranged for Katie to be seen by a pediatric hematologist/oncologist sympathetic to their cause so her treatment could be started as soon as possible. Once that was done, obtaining the chemotherapy drugs would be their next task. That would not be so easy.

His telephone rang on time, as expected. Matthew was on the other end of the line.

"Hi, Matthew. How did it go?"

"Well, Dr. Patrick, we got the girl but we also had some trouble." He filled in Dr. Patrick on the circumstances.

After a long pause, Dr. Patrick responded. "You did the right thing Matthew. It's probably better for the young boy. Is he stable for the time being?"

"He seems to be doing okay right now except for the pain."

"How is the little girl? It sounds like she's not handling things very well."

"Emily's doing her best, but she's pretty hysterical."

"How long before you get to St. Francis?"

"We should be there in about ten to fifteen minutes. Thomas is trying not to attract attention with his driving."

"That's smart. I'll call ahead and let Father Mark know about our second guest and get everything prepared in the likely event that the boy needs surgery."

Dr. Patrick gathered his thoughts, got several items together, and headed out the door. He made several calls on his way to St. Francis, including one to a longtime friend of his, a retired anesthesiologist. The treatment room at the safe house had been used to repair many minor injuries but never for a major operation. Although that made Patrick a bit nervous, he had operated in far worse conditions on some of his medical missions in Third World countries.

He considered trying to return the boy to one of the hospitals, but that would expose his team to unwanted questions and probable arrest. If the boy needed surgery, it would have to be performed by him.

The next issue would be dealing with Lieutenant Osgood. Hopefully he wouldn't blame the Underground for his son. If he did, he might change his mind about Katie and then use the enforcement unit to increase the pressure on the Underground itself.

Dr. Patrick arrived at St. Francis and quickly headed to the safe house. Thomas and his team had arrived shortly before him and were waiting for him. They had taken the boy to the treatment room and Emily was with the girl in one of the small side rooms.

As Dr. Patrick headed back to the treatment room, he heard the little girl quietly whimpering. The injured boy was conscious but clearly gravely injured.

"Young man, I'm Dr. Patrick. What's your name?"

The boy moaned and then quietly said, "Joshua."

"Well Joshua, I need to examine you to see how we can help you."

"Where's my sister?"

"She's in another room and she's okay. We don't want to hurt you or your sister. We are actually here to help her, but right now we have to take care of you."

Dr. Patrick examined Joshua and then turned to Thomas and asked him to prepare the room for surgery. He also had him start an IV and check Joshua's blood count.

Within a half hour, the room was ready and Joshua had received a liter of IV fluids and a dose of antibiotics. His blood pressure was better with the fluid but he was still pale. His blood count came back with a hemoglobin that was dangerously low. Luckily, his blood type matched Matthew's and Father Mark's. While they waited for the anesthesiologist, each of them donated blood in an adjacent room.

Dr. Patrick knew it would be useful if he had some assistance once he started the operation. Although Thomas and the others were helpful with getting things ready, he knew they would not be as useful during surgery. Emily came in as he was thinking about this.

"Have you ever been in an operating room, Emily?"

"I'm afraid not. I don't know if I could handle it. What about JP? I know he's just a medical student but he would be more helpful."

"That's a good idea, Emily but I'm not sure if he could come on such short notice or if he even wants to be involved."

"You know him a lot better than I do, Dr. Patrick, but I think he would come."

"I guess it won't hurt to try."

Dr. Patrick placed a call to JP and filled him in on the situation.

"So, what do you think, JP? Think you're ready for this?"

"I don't know. I still haven't come to terms with what you guys are doing."

"Well it's obviously up to you. I could definitely use some help and Emily thought you might be able to help me. I have the patient stabilized for the moment, but I have to move fast."

At the sound of her name, JP's interest perked up noticeably. "Emily suggested me?"

"Yes. I hadn't even really considered calling you until she suggested it."

"I'm coming. I'll need directions."

"The basement of St. Francis Church. We're in the safe house here. Please hurry."

※ ※ ※

Lieutenant Osgood arrived at the scene of the kidnapping and shooting within fifteen minutes of the call from his wife. The police were questioning his wife while his other children were sitting in the van. Janet gave him a hug as he walked up to her. He showed the detectives his badge and asked if he could speak to his wife alone for a minute. They reluctantly agreed and stepped back to their squad car where they checked the lieutenant's credentials on their computer.

Once alone, Janet filled in her husband on what had happened as she and Katie exited the pizza store. She was surprised at how calm Jaye was about Katie, but shaken about Joshua.

"How bad did Josh look when they took him?"

"I can't really say," Janet replied. "It all happened so fast—within seconds—I just don't know."

"Okay, honey, I'm sure they'll be fine. We'll find them. Don't tell the police anything about Katie's condition. I don't want them turning this over to the MEU."

"What are you talking about?" Janet replied angrily. "How do you know they'll be fine? Don't you think your team should be investigating this now?"

"I'll explain it all to you when we get home. Just do what I'm asking. You have to trust me right now," the lieutenant said, trying to sound convincing.

After hearing about Joshua, he himself was wondering whether he had made a big mistake in talking to the Underground. Now instead of losing one child, they might lose two.

The couple walked over to the police squad car. The officers had verified that the lieutenant's badge was indeed authentic and proceeded to take the rest of Janet's statement. As directed by her husband, she did not mention Katie's condition. Since the police assumed this was a regular kidnapping, they informed the Osgoods that the matter would be turned over to the FBI immediately and that they should expect a visit from them later in the evening.

❈ ❈ ❈

Captain Jameson left the office and headed to Sam's apartment. They were supposed to go out for dinner. As he drove, he again began thinking about the lieutenant's erratic behavior recently, as well as this news of his kids' abductions. The more he thought about it, the more something didn't sound right. Could the lieutenant be involved in illegal activity? That might explain why someone might kidnap his kids. Could he be the one leaking information from the Ministry of Health? That too would explain some of the problems in the enforcement unit.

As he arrived at Sam's, he was still pondering the various possibilities.

She came almost skipping out of her apartment and said, "I'm all yours tonight. I don't have any urgent studying for tomorrow."

The captain responded somewhat half-heartedly. "That's great."

"Well, don't jump for joy or anything," Sam said with a little pout on her face.

"What did you say?"

"Hello. Are you there?"

"I'm sorry, Sam. I am a little distracted. I'll tell you about it over dinner. I could use an unbiased person's perspective."

"I'll be happy to give my thoughts, but then you have to promise me to forget about work for the rest of the evening."

"I can't promise, but I'll do my best."

"I'll have to see what I can do to take your mind off it," she said with an inviting look on her face.

"I like the sound of that," he replied as they drove off.

※ ※ ※

JP arrived just as the anesthesiologist was putting Joshua out in the treatment room. For a makeshift operating room, he was amazed at how it looked. If he hadn't known better, he would have thought he was in an operating room at a hospital. It even had a hospital's antiseptic smell.

A big man dressed in a sterile gown was getting some instruments ready for the surgery. JP's grandfather was standing by the head of the bed, gently stroking the injured boy's shoulder and telling him he was going to be all right.

"Hi, Grandpa. I tried to get here as quickly as I could."

"You're just in time. We're just getting started. I know you haven't had much surgical experience yet, but I thought you could at least assist me. My eyes aren't what they used to be."

"I'll do whatever you tell me."

"Okay. This is the young boy that was accidentally shot in the abdomen while we were extracting his sister. I'm not sure about the extent of the injury, but more than likely some of his bowel may need to be removed. Since he's reasonably stable, I doubt any major blood vessels or his liver or spleen were hit. We'll know soon – let's get scrubbed."

❀ ❀ ❀

The lieutenant pulled into his driveway behind his wife's minivan and followed his wife and sons into the house. Janet proceeded to get the pizza ready for the kids as though nothing was wrong. He helped her silently and had the kids get washed for dinner. Once the pizza was served, he and Janet went out on the back deck of the house.

Her demeanor changed immediately. "What's going on, Jaye?"

The lieutenant told her everything. He said that he assumed the abduction had been executed by the Underground. However, he could not explain why they would have taken Joshua. Hesitantly, he added, "I'm sure if they have the means to get Katie treated, they probably have the means to treat Joshua."

"How could you do this without telling me?" Janet asked, almost screaming the question. "You may have caused us to lose two of our children!"

"I had to do something, Janet. I couldn't just sit by and let Katie be taken to the Center."

"I know, Jaye, but you should have discussed it with me."

"I'm sorry, honey. I just kind of reacted without thinking." He decided this would not be a good time to tell her that Katie would probably not be returned to them, even if her treatment were successful.

"It's okay. I just want you to know we're in this together."

※ ※ ※

Sam listened intently as Captain Jameson explained his concerns about Lieutenant Osgood and about what had happened earlier in the day. The restaurant was quiet and their table was in a corner, which made their conversation both easy and private.

"Why would anyone want to abduct his kids, let alone shoot one of them?"

"I've been told the shooting was accidental. Some wannabe cop thought he was going to be a hero and prevent a kidnapping. They have him in custody already. As to the motive for the kidnapping, I haven't the foggiest idea. I'm guessing Jaye could be into other things like drugs or gambling. Perhaps he owes some people some money. Maybe its extortion. But none of that seems to fit Jaye."

"Whatever it is, I would say it's personal. Dad wouldn't tell me anything about his meeting with the lieutenant. He just said he thought he was a good man."

"Well, I wouldn't expect him to say much more. Hopefully the FBI can shed a little light on what's going on when they get a handle on this kidnapping."

"Why is the FBI getting involved? Wouldn't the city detectives handle it?"

"The FBI handles all abductions, unless there are other extenuating circumstances."

"Well, hopefully they can quell your worries about the lieutenant," Sam said as she sipped the last of her drink. "Excuse me for a second, Mike."

As Sam headed to the restroom, the captain's cell phone rang. A pediatrician from the hospital had been patched through to him.

"This is Captain Jameson. How may I help you, Doctor?"

"Sir, I am a pediatrician at the hospital clinic. In my capacity there, I have been seeing the Osgood children. I just heard about the abduction of two of the Osgood children on the news, including a little girl named Katie. I thought it was my duty to report to you that we recently diagnosed her as having a form of leukemia that the Act deems non-treatable. I remember the case clearly because her father became quite irate when I told them there was nothing to do for her. In fact, I thought he was going to hit me. I don't know if it had anything to do with her abduction, but it made me wonder if the Underground is involved. At any rate, I hope I did the right thing by notifying you."

"Absolutely, Doctor. Thank you very much." The captain hung up his cell phone just as Sam returned to the table. "Well, it turns out that the lieutenant's little girl may have been abducted by the Underground. Her pediatrician just informed me that she has leukemia, a form not treatable under today's guidelines. That could sure explain his behavior lately. "

"No kidding. But how would the Underground have found out about her condition?"

"I'm not sure, but they seem to have their ways. At least now we have some jurisdiction in the case. I can have my guys start looking into it, along with the FBI. I'll have to meet with your father tomorrow and fill him in."

"This may seem far-fetched, but... you don't think the lieutenant would have arranged the abduction do you?"

"That's an interesting thought, Sam. I knew bouncing things

off of you was a good idea."

"You'd think someone in his position would realize that his daughter would have to go to the End of Life Care Center. Although, if he's the involved father you've said, he might just look for another option for his little girl."

"You might just be on to something, Sam." He leaned over and gave her a kiss. "I think you do have a future in the MEU."

※ ※ ※

JP's pulse raced as he scrubbed for surgery with his grandfather. He had been in plenty of ORs and ERs as an observer, and he had worked on many medical cadavers. But he was still too early in his medical training for hands-on experience with live patients.

Matthew helped JP and Dr. Patrick don sterile gowns and gloves. Dr. Patrick approached the makeshift operating table and marked out an incision, starting in the middle of Joshua's abdomen from just above the pubic bone, up and around the belly button. JP stepped up to the table and gingerly placed his hands on the abdomen, to avoid contaminating his sterile gloves.

JP was amazed as he watched the deft hands of his eighty-year-old grandfather meticulously explore the abdomen of young Joshua. The bullet had entered the abdomen and luckily had missed the aorta and vena cava. Unfortunately, it had traversed two loops of his small intestine and blood was steadily oozing from the blood vessels supplying the bowel. JP retracted as his grandfather attempted to control the bleeding. Dr. Patrick clamped and tied several bleeders but not before the anesthesiologist noted that Joshua's blood pressure had again dropped. More blood was given quickly and the pressure returned to normal. Dr. Patrick then proceeded to remove the sections of bowel that had been injured. His hands moved with grace and ease as he sewed the first section of the bowel back together.

"This is the old-fashioned way, JP."

Numerous stapling devices were available to repair the bowel but not in this improvised operating room. As his grandfather was sewing the second loop of bowel, JP noticed the old man's hands start to shake.

"Everything okay, Grandpa?"

"Sure, JP. I just don't have the stamina for this anymore."

Once the bowel repair was completed, Dr. Patrick looked around the abdomen one final time to make sure he hadn't missed any other injury. Assured that he hadn't, he irrigated the abdominal cavity with warm saline and began to close it. After closing the first layer, Dr. Patrick handed JP the needle holder and showed him how to close the skin.

"Are you sure I should be doing this?"

"Now's as good a time as any. Besides, these old hands are tired. I think you'll do just fine."

JP had not had the chance to sew real skin yet, but had practiced on pig's feet. Dr. Patrick smiled to himself as he watched his grandchild put his first few sutures into a real person. It was a moment he still remembered from back when he was a medical student.

Once the incision was closed and the dressing was in place, the anesthesiologist allowed Joshua to awaken. He woke up calmly, but was in obvious pain. They subsequently moved him to one of the side rooms where he would be monitored closely for the next few days.

JP beamed as he broke scrub and removed his gloves and sterile gown. It had been his first real operation and one that he would surely never forget. He washed his hands and then followed Dr. Patrick and their young patient back to the boy's room. Dr.

Patrick filled in Matthew on how to monitor the boy and made sure everything was satisfactory before retiring to the front room of the safe house. JP also returned to the front room, where he found Father Mark and Emily sitting and talking.

"Will he be all right, John?" Father Mark asked as they entered.

"Barring any complications, I think he'll be just fine. How's our other little guest doing, Emily?"

"I think she's scared to death, Dr. Patrick, but she did finally fall asleep."

"At her age, it's gonna be hard for her to understand what's going on. Hopefully, she'll calm down and we can get her to trust us. Otherwise, it's gonna be hard for her and us. I think you'll play an important role in earning her trust, Emily."

"I'll do my best. What's the next step for her, Doctor?" Emily asked.

"We'll give her a few days to get used to us and then we'll have the pediatric oncologist see her, to get her treatment started."

"What about her brother?" Father Mark asked. "How will we get him back to his parents?"

"I'm going to have to give that some more thought, Father. Right now I'll just concentrate on getting him well."

Dr. Patrick looked over at JP and continued, "What do you think about our little operation now? Are you still undecided about helping us now and then?"

"I'm in it now whether I want to be or not. But just for the record, I couldn't think of a better group than this one."

They all smiled at that answer just as Matthew entered the front room. "Dr. Patrick, the boy is fully awake now and is asking where he is and if his sister is okay."

"I'll be right there, Matthew. JP, why don't you head home? I think I'm going to stay here and keep an eye on our patients tonight."

"Actually Grandpa, I'm hungry. Anybody interested in getting a little dinner?"

Father Mark and Dr. Patrick both said they would eat something there, but Emily accepted JP's offer, just as he had hoped. Dr. Patrick gave a sly wink to JP as he and Emily headed out the door.

✳ ✳ ✳

Sam and Captain Jameson finished dinner and were just leaving as JP and Emily entered the restaurant. Both Sam and JP were surprised by the chance encounter.

"Hi, Sam. Taking the night off from studying?"

"Yeah. Looks like you're playing hooky, too," she retorted jokingly. "You remember Captain Jameson. You briefly met in the library a while back."

"Nice to see you again, Captain."

"Please, call me Mike."

"Are you going to introduce us to your friend?" Sam asked, nodding at Emily.

JP looked over at Emily somewhat sheepishly and noticed Emily's face was ashen. He took her hand and she relaxed a little but he could feel the tension in her. "This is Emily, a friend of mine from Grandpa's church. He introduced us a few weeks ago. This is Sam, one of my classmates, and Captain Mike Jameson, her friend."

"Nice to meet you, Emily," Sam replied. "Have we met before? You look so familiar."

JP felt Emily's hand tense again. "No, I'm sure we haven't met. But it's nice to meet the both of you now."

"You probably just look like someone else I know. I'm bad

with names but pretty good with faces. Oh, well, again, it is nice to meet you. Watch out for this guy, he's a wild one," Sam added as she headed out the door with the captain.

"Thanks, Sam. I'll get you back for that one," JP bantered back as the door closed.

JP and Emily were shown to a table.

"Sorry about that, Emily. Who would have thought we would run into the captain of the Medical Enforcement Unit? Anyway, you handled it just fine. Sam's a good girl. I wouldn't worry about her."

"That's okay, I guess I'm going to have to get used to being out in public again without freaking out. Now... just how wild are you?" she said with a relaxed smile.

23

LIEUTENANT OSGOOD WAS ON his way to work, wondering just how much longer he would have a job. He didn't know why he had been so stupid to think that he could circumvent the system. Now, instead of one child in trouble, he had two. Not only that, how was he going to explain the situation to the captain? Lieutenant Osgood considered trying to contact the Underground again to find out about Joshua, but he knew that would be too risky. He'd have to wait for the Underground to contact him. And he figured it was almost a certainty that Captain Jameson would have him under surveillance.

As soon as he arrived at the office, Osgood was told the captain wanted to see him in the office. No surprise. He walked to the office and Captain Jameson waved him in.

"Jaye, why didn't you tell me Katie was sick? I felt terrible when her pediatrician called me after he heard about her abduction. I knew you had been acting funny but I had no idea it was about your little girl. I'm very sorry."

The lieutenant breathed a sigh of relief at the captain's concern. "Thanks, Captain. The whole thing's been a nightmare for Janet and me. We've been in a state of shock since we found out. Katie looks so healthy and yet they say she has a non-treatable cancer. It just doesn't make any sense. And now, with Joshua being shot, we just don't know what to do."

"Have you heard anything from the kidnappers yet?"

"Nothing at all."

"Well, rest assured we'll find them and we'll get the people responsible for this. We take care of our own."

"Thanks, Captain. I'm sorry I've been so distracted. But my wife and I have been preparing ourselves to, you know, what the Act requires. But putting your own child to death, is..." The lieutenant covered his eyes with his hand for a moment. "I'm sorry, Captain, for not being more forthcoming sooner. We were just holding out hope that maybe the diagnosis was wrong or that other treatment options might be available. She's our little girl, sir, our baby."

"Don't worry about it, Jaye. You've got enough to worry about. Why don't you take a few days off and let us handle this? I'll let you know if we find out anything."

"Thank you, Captain. I'm sure Janet will appreciate me being home."

The lieutenant left the captain's office and headed straight for his car. It appeared as though Jameson didn't suspect his involvement with the abduction, yet.

24

DR. PATRICK WAS PLEASED with Joshua's progress. He never ceased to be amazed by the resiliency of children. It had only been a few days and Joshua was already up walking around and almost back on a regular diet. Once he was feeling better, they let him see Katie. It perked him up tremendously to see that his little sister was safe. It also helped Katie, who was now a little calmer in her new environment.

Joshua was in visiting his sister when Dr. Patrick arrived to make rounds on his two young patients. He was happy to find them together and at the same time it saddened him that they would soon be separated, perhaps permanently.

"Good morning, Josh, Katie. How are you guys?"

"I wanna go see Mommy," Katie whimpered.

"We'll go home soon, Katie," Joshua quickly responded in a reassuring voice. "I'm feeling just fine, Doctor."

"That's great, Joshua. I'm glad to see you're keeping your little sister company. I'm sure that makes her feel much better. How old are you, Joshua?"

"I'm thirteen."

"Well, I'd say that was very brave of you to jump out of the van to help your sister. You're a courageous young man and a very good big brother."

Joshua beamed with pride. "Thank you, Doctor."

"Now, if you could, I need to have you come with me, Josh. I have another doctor friend of mine who needs to check Katie. We'll just go out to the front room. Emily will come in to be with Katie while the doctor examines her. Is that okay with you?"

The boy leaned over to Katie and told her he would be just down the hall. As he and Dr. Patrick headed to the door, Emily knocked and came walking in with a little teddy bear for Katie.

"Hi, Katie. Look who I found outside, looking for a friend."

Katie smiled and held out her hands to accept the bear. Dr. Patrick knew Katie was in good hands with Emily who seemed to have a great way with children. Dr. Benjamin Jonason arrived on schedule. He was short and stocky, reminding Dr. Patrick of a Hobbit from Tolkien's classic trilogy, *The Lord of The Rings*. The only thing not Hobbit-like about him was the permanent scowl on his face. Despite his gruff appearance, he had a very gentle bedside manner as well as a heart of gold. He was a brilliant hematologist and oncologist who happened to believe that doctors should be allowed to compassionately treat all patients. Dr. Jonason had helped the Underground on several occasions.

Dr. Patrick introduced Dr. Jonason to Joshua and then showed him to Katie's room. After introducing him to Emily and Katie, Dr. Patrick returned to the front room, where the worried Joshua waited.

"He's not going to hurt Katie, is he?"

"No, Joshua. He's a very good doctor and he's gonna try to help your sister. I'm not sure if your parents told you or not, but Katie's sick, and that's why we brought her here. We can give her special medicine and care. You, on the other hand, were not supposed to be brought here. Your injury was an accident. But we brought you here too so that you could get treated fast."

"Who are you guys?" Joshua asked. "Why didn't my parents just take Katie to the doctor at the hospital for help?"

"Well, Joshua, that's a little more difficult to explain." Dr. Patrick decided it was too much for him to understand and that it might cause friction between Joshua and his dad. "Let me just say the doctors at the hospital weren't able to help Katie so we decided to try and help instead."

"But who are you guys anyway? Does my dad know you?" Joshua persisted.

"I can't tell you that, Joshua. I can only say we are a bunch of people who like to help other people whenever we can. You might ask your dad to explain that to you when you get home." Joshua appeared to accept that answer, so Dr. Patrick approached the next subject. "Now, Joshua, I need to talk about getting you back home to your family."

"You mean you're going to take Katie and me home soon?"

"Well, it's not as simple as that, Joshua. We can't just take you straight home though we will get you back to your parents. But..." Dr. Patrick wasn't sure how Joshua was going handle this next part. "...Katie is going to have to stay here with us for the time being, so we can help her get well."

Joshua looked down at the floor for a couple of minutes and then asked, "Will she ever be able to come home, Doctor?"

"Perhaps, Joshua," Dr. Patrick answered, stunned by his youthful wisdom. Dr. Patrick never wanted to deny hope to anyone. Over his many years of surgery, he had noticed that patients who gave up hope seemed to die more quickly of their disease than did those who did not, especially if that hope involved a higher power.

"But in the meantime, we have to get you ready to go home. We're working on that now."

Dr. Jonason returned from Katie's room at that point and Dr. Patrick motioned for Joshua to rejoin his sister.

"What do you think, Ben?"

"She looks healthy right now, but obviously looks can be deceiving at this stage. The first thing I want to do is review her blood smears. It wouldn't be the first case I've seen that was misinterpreted by the government lab. Is there any chance we could get the original slides, or will we have to get new ones?"

"I'm not sure, Ben. The only information we have right now is what we shared with you. If the diagnosis is correct, what's her prognosis?"

"I would say fifty-fifty if we can get her the appropriate chemo."

"I'd say that's better than no chance at the End of Life Care Center."

"You got that, John."

"I'll see what my sources can do and be in touch with you in a day or two. Thanks for the visit."

"My pleasure, John."

25

CAPTAIN JAMESON WAS FRUSTRATED by the lack of progress on the lieutenant's case. The few leads they'd had all led to
dead ends. He hadn't talked to the lieutenant in several days but
thought it was time to ask him some more questions. He was on
his way to the lieutenant's home to talk to him. He also hoped
that Osgood's wife might be able to shed a little light on what
had been going on. He thought that Katie's illness and abduction
probably explained the lieutenant's recent behavior, but still,
something just didn't seem to fit. How did the Underground find
out about Katie so quickly and why did he seem more worried
about Joshua than he did Katie?

At the Osgood residence, Captain Jameson was greeted at the
door by the lieutenant. "Captain, I'm surprised to see you here.
Did you find my kids?

"No, no."

"Oh, I'm sorry, sir. Come on in. When I saw you unexpectedly
like this, I thought maybe you were here to report something. I
got ahead of myself." He turned and announced to Janet that the

captain was there.

She came hurriedly out of the kitchen and without a word of welcome said, "Did you find Josh and Katie?"

"No, honey. I already asked."

"I'm sorry, Captain," she said. "I've been a nervous wreck since the kids were taken. It all happened so suddenly. One minute I was getting a pizza and the next Joshua is shot and he and Katie are taken from me."

"That's okay, Janet, and please call me Mike," the captain replied. "We're doing everything we can to find them. Have you heard anything from the kidnappers?"

"Nothing at all," Jaye said as he offered the captain a seat in the living room.

"Well, it's not unusual for the Underground to remain quiet. Their goal is to rescue and treat those not salvageable and they really don't care how they do it."

Janet cringed as the captain used the term *not salvageable*. "So, Captain—I mean Mike—you think the Underground is behind this? You think this has something to do with Katie's cancer?" Janet asked, pretending to be surprised.

"Yes, Janet. I wasn't aware of it until your pediatrician called me after the kidnapping. That's what made us shift our investigation toward the Underground."

"That makes sense, but why our child? They would have to know stealing the child of an MEU officer would really antagonize the Unit," Janet said with a furtive glance at her husband. "And how would they even have found out about Katie?"

"Those are some of the same questions we're trying to get answers to, Janet," the captain said. "So how are the other boys holding up? Are they aware of what's going on with Katie and Joshua?"

Janet was curious about the sudden shift in the captain's concern for their kids. She didn't know if he actually cared or if he was just making conversation. She instinctively didn't trust him and thought he was really at their house for an ulterior reason. Since taking over as the head of the MEU, he had never shown any interest in Jaye or the family, so she doubted that his concern was sincere.

"They're doing okay. They think they're just gone from home for a while, visiting grandparents. They don't understand the gravity of the situation."

"That's probably for the better," Captain Jameson replied.

"So, Captain. Is there something we can do for you?" Janet asked, deciding to cut to the chase.

"No, not really, I just hadn't touched base with you and Jaye for several days, so I decided to come by and see how you were doing. There is something that has been needling me since the kidnapping, but I just can't seem to put my finger on it. Is there anything else you can tell me that may be useful?"

Janet again nervously looked over at her husband and then responded. "No, we've exhausted ourselves trying to think of anything that might bring the kids home, but there's nothing. All we have are questions."

"Mom, Dad, where are you? We can't get the movie started."

Jaye jumped up and said, "Sorry, Captain, I'll be right back."

As the lieutenant left the room, Captain Jameson decided to take advantage of being alone with Janet.

"Has it been good having Jaye home during this time, Janet?"

Janet seemed almost startled by the question, but composed herself and answered, "Absolutely, Captain. Thank you so much for letting him have some time off. It's been a great help around here with the other boys."

He could see her hands shaking as he continued. "How are you really doing, Janet?"

"Honestly, I'm worried sick. I want my kids back. I want to know if my son is alive."

"What about Katie? I've noticed neither one of you seem to be worried about her. That seems a little odd to me."

"Well, uhhhh. I guess we assumed, like you, that the Underground kidnapped her and that she's probably being treated well."

"But you understand that they are criminals, don't you?"

"Of course, Captain."

"And that working with them or protecting them is illegal?"

"Working with whom?" Jaye asked as he walked back into the room and noticed his wife visibly shaken.

"Oh, we were just talking about the Underground. Nothing new to you. Well, listen, I need to get back to the office. I'm glad you two are staying strong. I'll let you know as soon as we find out anything."

Jaye showed the captain to the door and watched him drive off. When he closed the door, Janet said, "I think he knows what you did for Katie. I tried to act confused about why the Underground would target Katie, but I don't think he believed me. I don't think he believes us."

"How could he know? I think he was just fishing. We have to stay calm. I'll head back to work soon and everything will be fine."

Janet turned and went to the kitchen, still obviously shaken by her encounter with the captain. Jaye wondered to himself if Janet was right, but thought he would have been arrested already. No, everything was still on course. The ballgame wasn't over yet.

※ ※ ※

The captain drove back to his office, convinced the Osgoods were lying. Janet was definitely hiding something. It was time to add more surveillance on the lieutenant. Osgood could have been the leak in his organization all along.

26

DR. PATRICK WAS UNSURE how to contact the lieutenant. He knew it would be difficult to make arrangements to get Joshua home. They could just drop him off close to home and let him walk the rest of the way, but he figured the whole area would be under surveillance. The exchange would have to take place elsewhere. He would go through the informants and try to arrange a neutral drop-off area.

He was waiting for Dr. Jonason to show up at his house to talk about Katie. Jonason had good news about her condition and wanted to discuss options for her in person.

Dr. Jonason came walking in with a definite bounce to his step. His short legs were moving faster than usual and, unusually, he was smiling. Dr. Patrick showed him in to the living room.

"Can I get you something to drink, Ben?"

"No, no, John. I have to get back to the office, but I couldn't wait to talk to you about our little patient. I got the slides of her bone marrow biopsy and reviewed them. They were right about her having leukemia, but I believe they were wrong about the subtype. I took the liberty of anonymously sending her slides to a friend of mine and he agreed. The type she has should be easily treatable with chemotherapy alone, with a greater than ninety-percent potential for success."

"That's great Ben. They were going to terminate that child without even a second opinion. It's unconscionable if you ask me."

"Well, before you get too excited, there is one potential problem. It may take some doing to get the chemotherapy drugs that I'll need to treat her. Those drugs are closely monitored by the Ministry of Health."

"We'll just have to figure out a way. I'm not going to let bureaucratic red tape kill this little girl."

"I'll leave that up to you, but I can give you a list of what she needs. Just let me know if you're successful and I'll get started with her treatment."

Dr. Patrick warmly shook his friend's hand. "Okay, Ben. Thanks for all your help."

Dr. Jonason left a list of the chemotherapeutic drugs he would need to treat Katie and then headed back to his office. With his renewed sense of hope for Katie, Dr. Patrick got right to work. He was anxious to start planning the next steps.

27

AFTER HIS FIRST ENCOUNTER with the MEU lieutenant, Steve really didn't want to mess with him again. Times were tough, though, and he could really use a little money. This time he had just left a message for the lieutenant, so he hoped it would be much less involved and less risky. Steve had also arranged to meet him at a different location this time, to avoid any run-ins with his former business partners.

The park was full of activity. The weather was much warmer than usual and the sun was shining. Steve was in a jogging suit, although he had no intention of jogging. He never exerted himself unnecessarily.

He had arranged to meet the lieutenant on a bridge over a small stream that ran through the park. He slowly walked out on it and peered down at the running stream. As the water babbled peacefully beneath him, he thought about his simple life and wondered why anyone would want to work. His philosophy had always been to do just enough to survive, even if it meant going hungry once in a while. He couldn't imagine what drove people to work their lives away. Whatever it was, he didn't want any part of it.

A hand was placed on his left shoulder and his daydreaming was interrupted. Lieutenant Osgood was standing next to him.

"Hello Steve. I hope we don't have to jump through more hoops before we get down to business this time."

"No, no. I won't play any games with you. I just have information to give."

"Fine then, tell me and be on your way. I don't want to prolong this any more than I have to."

"They'd like you to know that your son is fine and they want to arrange for him to be transferred back to you."

Lieutenant Osgood was so elated at the news he almost wanted to hug the lowlife in front of him. However, his thoughts returned to the matter at hand. He hadn't given any thought to how to get Joshua returned to them, but now realized it was not a simple matter. Once Joshua came back, Osgood knew there were be a lot of questioning by his own people at the Ministry. He hated the thought that his boy would have to undergo such intense interrogation right after having gone through such an ordeal.

There was danger to everyone involved. If anyone was with Joshua, they would be instantly arrested and the penalties would be steep. Therefore a pickup would have to be carefully arranged.

"That's great. We will have to arrange a neutral drop-off area to decrease the risk to all of us."

"Is that all you want me to pass on?"

"That's all and tell them thanks. Is there any word on Katie?"

"They didn't say anything about a girl. I'll pass on your reply." Steve turned and slowly walked away. He put his hands back behind his head as though he had just finished running and was catching his breath. He could at least act the part.

✳ ✳ ✳

Captain Jameson listened as his officer recapped his reconnaissance on the lieutenant. He was finally getting somewhere on the case. His officer had followed the man Osgood met on the bridge in the park. He had found out the man's name was Steve Johnson and that he was a lazy, down and out, streetwise informant who subsisted on selling information to the highest bidder. Amazingly, Steve's police record was limited, with only a couple of counts of disorderly conduct and public drunkenness. He had never held down a full-time job, so there was little information about him, other than that he seemed to have contacts on both sides of the law.

The captain was sure they could use this Steve Johnson to get to better targets, such as the local players in the Underground and perhaps even his own second-in-command. He leaned back in his chair and smiled. The situation was looking brighter and his career was looking more and more secure.

28

JP WAS ON HIS way to his grandfather's house for yet another meeting of the Underground. Helping his grandfather during the surgery on Joshua had been the most exciting thing he had done since he'd started medical school. However, he still didn't know if he was cut out for a cloak and dagger life. If he decided against it, the government would control what he would be doing in the future, but at least he would be doing good for some people. If he continued to assist the Underground, he might not even be able to graduate. One false move and it would be all over.

On the other hand, there were his grandfather and Emily to consider. His grandfather had seemed so proud of JP when he assisted him with Joshua. How could he possibly let the old man down? Also, what would Emily think of him if he backed out now? He had grown fond of her and didn't want to disappoint her. What he really wanted was to spend a lot more time with her. That also would put him at increased risk, regardless of whether he helped the Underground or not.

JP entered his grandfather's house and was surprised to see

only Emily and his grandfather present. He thought for a moment that he had come too early but looked at his watch and realized he was actually a few minutes late.

"Where's the rest of the gang?"

"Actually, you and Emily are the only two I called in for this meeting."

"I thought you had some mission in mind so I expected everyone to be here."

The doctor ushered his guests into the kitchen and they all sat around his breakfast table. "In this case, you and Emily are the only ones needed for the mission," he said. He quickly brought them up to speed on the details of Katie's abduction. He then explained that Katie's leukemia had been found to be treatable. "The only problem is getting the chemotherapy meds to treat her. We initially thought we might be able to raid a supply shipment. Unfortunately, no shipments are planned for some time, so the only place we'll be able to obtain the drugs is the hospital."

It dawned on him why he had been asked to be part of the mission. JP started shaking his head.

"You can't possibly think we can steal the drugs from the hospital do you?"

"Well, actually, I do."

Emily had remained quiet up to this point, but it was clear that JP was going to need some convincing so it was her turn to talk.

"JP, we have to do this. Katie is only five years old. If we don't help her, she will die one way or the other; either from her disease or in the morgue. After almost ending up there myself, I, for one, will do whatever it takes to help her."

As Emily spoke, Dr. Patrick noticed how JP seemed mesmerized by her. He suspected this fascination might motivate his grandson to participate, although he really hoped he would come around just on the merits of the mission. He wanted JP to help for Katie's sake—not just to please Emily.

JP was struggling with it all. "Now that you know she was misdiagnosed, why can't you just turn her back over to the hospital and get her treated there?"

"That is a good question, JP and we did consider that. However, we thought it might prompt questioning that could lead them to Dr. Jonason. He's a valuable asset to the Underground and that option was ruled out."

"You do realize my med school career will be over if we're caught?"

"Of course I do, JP, but there's no other way. It could be months before another shipment is sent. Katie needs her treatment now. Her best chance of successful treatment is when the disease is in its early stages."

JP hadn't expected to come to such a crossroads so early in his life. Career choices were hard enough at this stage. Many of his friends had already had several different jobs or had changed majors in college multiple times. He had gone straight through with one goal in mind—to become a doctor. Now he was facing a choice that could change everything, and he didn't know if he was up to it. He got up and leaned against the kitchen counter in thought.

After several moments of silence, Dr. Patrick continued. "I know what you're going through JP. Everybody involved with the Underground has had to make similar decisions. Twenty to thirty years ago, I never expected to be spending my retirement doing this either, but the bottom line is, if good people remain silent and do nothing, only evil prevails. And if a little girl like Katie loses her life, evil has definitely prevailed!"

"Amen to that," Emily said. "You know, JP, before all this happened to me, I was so absorbed in my own problems with the OCD, I had no idea how much evil existed in the world. Now

I know that evil is real but more importantly, I know there are good people in the world also, like William who gave his life for mine. To me, the choice is simple, you think of yourself and let evil prevail, or you do what you can to make a difference."

Dr. Patrick thought that JP might be softening a little. He was glad Emily was helping out. She obviously was committed to the cause. But when someone lays down his life for you, what else would one expect? He decided it was time to play his final card with JP. "There is one more thing you need to know, JP, before you decide. How far back do you remember in your childhood?"

JP thought for a moment then replied with a confused look. "Like most people, I don't have many memories before I was four or five years old. How can that possibly be pertinent now?"

"I don't think your parents ever wanted you to know this, but when you were about two, your twin sister..." He took note of the look of shock on his grandson's face. "Yes, twin sister. She developed renal failure, following a strep infection. Although most post-strep renal failures are temporary, the Act had ended all dialysis treatment, even for reversible problems. She died from her renal failure before her kidneys turned around."

JP still looked stunned. "You're telling me I had a twin sister?"

"That's correct, JP. That's the main reason I decided I had to become more involved. Believe me, I wanted to just fade off into retirement and resume some of my traveling. Annie was my catalyst. I had to do something about a system that was inherently evil."

JP's legs were shaking and he sat back down.

"I'm sorry to have to be the one to tell you this but it was a time that changed all of us. Your parents were so devastated they never really recovered. Their way of dealing with their grief was to develop something of a defeatist attitude and just go along with the status quo, mostly for your benefit."

Emily pulled her chair next to JP's and held his hand. He remained quiet and stared down at the floor. After several minutes of silence, he finally looked up at his grandfather and said, "What do you want us to do?"

29

AFTER THE MEETING WITH Steve in the park, a handoff scenario had been arranged by the Underground. Lieutenant Osgood felt comfortable about the meeting, but was worried about Joshua's safety.

He had decided to tell no one about Joshua's impending return, not even his wife. He figured the fewer people who knew, the better. That way, should the MEU be alerted, his wife would not be culpable. The lieutenant was not pleased that the arrangements had been made through a paid informant, but he understood the necessity. He had no choice but to trust that Steve was not playing both sides. If Steve did try to double-cross him, it would be his last time informing or breathing.

※ ※ ※

Matthew picked up Joshua at the safe house on schedule and was on his way to the drop-off point. The boy was not happy leaving his sister behind, but had been gently told he had no choice if he wanted her to get well. To avoid any possibility of leaving a trail to the safe house, they had been driving around the city for nearly half an hour. Joshua remained silent until Matthew broke the ice.

"Are you anxious to get back home, Josh?"

"It would be better if Katie were coming with me. I don't understand why she can't just go to the hospital and get her medicine."

"Well, Josh, a long time ago it used to be that way. But people lost sight of the fact that life was precious and a gift from God. Then people became more interested in how much medicine cost rather than the people it was treating."

Matthew knew this was too simplistic an explanation but hoped it would suffice for now. Joshua's next question, however, made him realize that the boy could probably understand much more.

"Does that mean my dad is a bad person since he works for the Medical Enforcement Unit?"

"Uhhhh, I don't think so, Josh. I think he's probably a good man who's just trying to provide for his family. Otherwise, I don't think he would have taken such a risk trying to get Katie treated by us. You can be proud of your father. I think he's doing what he thinks is best for all of you."

For the remainder of the drive, Joshua stared out the window silently and Matthew could only hope he hadn't said the wrong thing about Katie and Joshua's dad. The last thing he wanted was to alienate Josh from his father.

❊ ❊ ❊

Steve was not happy about having to snitch on the lieutenant, but what choice had he had? Shortly after he'd arranged the handoff meeting between the lieutenant and the Medical Underground, the enforcement unit had picked him up. The captain of the unit had made it very clear to him. He'd either cooperate or face conspiracy charges against the Medical Reconciliation Act. Steve's reputation as a merchant of information would be tarnished by snitching on the lieutenant, but a taint was better than prison. There were many people in prison because of information he had provided, so his life there might be short.

He had been told to stay away from the drop-off area so there would be no chance of being seen by the lieutenant. However, he couldn't resist seeing it all go down, especially since the lieutenant had been rough with him at their first meeting. In fact, Steve thought it would be entertaining.

Steve couldn't decide where would be the best place to stand to get the best view of the action. As he surveyed the area, he spotted a refreshment stand about twenty-five yards from the entrance to the Ferris wheel, where the exchange was to take place. It had picnic tables in front of it that allowed a direct view of the entrance. He decided to grab a bite to eat and watch the action unfold from there. A little popcorn to go with the movie, he chuckled to himself.

※ ※ ※

Matthew pulled his car to a stop outside the amusement park and told Joshua to stay in the car. He was about thirty minutes early and intended to check the area out before putting Joshua in harm's way again. As he'd expected, the park was busy, and that was a good thing. Dr. Patrick had picked the location specifically for that reason. If the MEU had gotten word about the drop-off, they would be less trigger-happy in a crowd of innocent bystanders than in an open park. Despite that, both Matthew and

Dr. Patrick were nervous. They trusted the lieutenant but had less faith in the informant.

After a good look around, Matthew left the amusement park and went back to the car. Joshua was patiently waiting for him as he had been told, waiting for the exact time he was to be at the Ferris wheel.

❋ ❋ ❋

The lieutenant entered the park and casually walked around the various amusement games. A shot rang out at the shooting gallery and he had his own gun halfway out before he realized it was just a game. He was on edge but he had to be careful, or he could ruin the drop-off or worse yet, get someone hurt or killed.

The lieutenant paced around the park, wondering what the future might hold for him, and began second-guessing his decision to contact the Underground in the first place. If he had done nothing, Joshua would not have gotten shot and his own job would not be in jeopardy. How had the country gotten to this point where parents had to make such decisions? It was too much for anyone.

❋ ❋ ❋

Captain Jameson had a small detail of officers spread out around the park in plain clothes. He knew the lieutenant would recognize the members of his usual tactical units, so Jameson had enlisted some of the security guards from the hospital and End of Life Care Center for this detail. He was sitting in an unmarked car with a direct view of the Ferris wheel, coordinating the operation. He smiled when he thought about how this bust would promote his career. When he'd first been assigned the position as captain of the enforcement unit, he had been concerned that it might be the end of his rise through the ranks. A major breakthrough in dealing with the Underground could propel him to higher positions; perhaps even a regional directorship or a Ministry position. In fact, he questioned why the Minister of Health had to be a doctor. After all, a nonmedical director would have less trouble making the tough calls when it came to life and death decisions.

❋ ❋ ❋

The lieutenant grew nervous as the arranged time drew near. As he walked through the park on his initial surveillance of the scene, he hadn't recognized anyone suspicious, but he just didn't trust Steve one little bit. However, for Joshua, he would take any risks and would just have to accept the consequences.

Strolling around the park, he acted like a regular family man on a day off with his kids. The only problem was that his children weren't with him, and that made him stick out like a sore thumb or, worse, a pervert looking for some prey. He had considered bringing one of the other boys with him, but with all that had gone on recently, he hadn't felt he could take that chance.

The time approached for the hand-off and he began walking to the Ferris wheel. As he neared it, his hand instinctively reached inside his jacket to the butt of his gun. It gave him a feeling of security he greatly needed. He knew that if this was a setup, his future was bleak. There would be little opportunity for escape and he would most likely end up in jail for a long, long time. He felt it was a small price to pay if Joshua was allowed to go home.

❋ ❋ ❋

Captain Jameson sat calmly in his vehicle. Things were going well. One of his men had spotted Lieutenant Osgood walking around the park, confirming that a drop was going down as the informant had stated. Now it was just a matter of time before Jameson's career would skyrocket. A bust like this could lead to even more arrests, perhaps of the big players in the region. His mouth watered at the thought of this. *Minister Jameson* had a good ring to it. He was sure Sam and her father would be quite impressed by his success. His asking for the minister's daughter's hand in marriage, which he was considering, would be a mere formality.

He radioed his men to wait at their posts until he gave the order to move in. He wanted both men and he wanted them with no resistance. An unwanted incident here in the amusement park would not help his plans for the future one bit. He picked up his binoculars and scanned the Ferris wheel area. His radio was tuned and ready to give the word to his men.

Things began to happen quickly. As the lieutenant approached the Ferris wheel entrance, he caught site of Joshua being escorted by a very large man. At the sight of his son, he was tempted to start running toward them but forced himself to remain calm to avoid any undue attention. Joshua looked great, and that alone raised Osgood's spirits and made him relax a little, something he would soon regret.

The man walking with Josh was one of the largest men Osgood had ever seen. He looked like a giant next to Josh and the lieutenant was sure he was a man not to mess with.

Captain Jameson had his radio in his hand but was waiting for the right moment to tighten the noose. He noticed a large man, accompanied by a boy, heading toward the Ferris wheel. Jameson had never met the lieutenant's son, but had seen recent pictures of him. He was pretty sure this was the target. Soon, his patience would be rewarded and his future would look much brighter.

Matthew spotted the lieutenant about the same time that Joshua caught sight of him. Josh started to run to his father but was held back by Matthew's large hand.

"Just a minute, Josh. We have to do this slowly. We don't want anything to go wrong." Matthew scanned the surroundings again and saw nothing suspicious. He continued the approach toward the lieutenant, who had stopped at the entrance to the Ferris wheel. So far, so good.

Captain Jameson watched as the two men approached each other. He wanted them together before he radioed his men to move in all at once. This would make it easier to cordon off the area, avoiding any mishaps with innocent bystanders and making escape much more difficult. "Just a little bit more," he mumbled to himself—

He jumped up as he watched one of his men, Officer Longley, approaching the two men. "What the hell?" Longley was new to the MEU and hadn't seen much action.

Jameson keyed his radio to try and stop Longley, but it was too late. The big man leading the lieutenant's son spotted him and saw the officer's Glock come out of his coat. Jameson had no choice now. "All men move in, NOW!" The captain began running toward the Ferris wheel entrance.

Matthew saw a man approaching from the direction of the shooting gallery. At first he was not concerned, but as he got closer, the man reached into his coat and Matthew saw the butt end of a pistol. Matthew froze momentarily, but decided he had no choice but to run. He knew Joshua would be okay since his father was close by. He let go of Josh's hand and turned and started running toward the back of the amusement park.

The lieutenant was caught off-guard by the sudden change in the situation. He had been so focused on Joshua that he hadn't noticed the man approaching from the shooting gallery. Obviously the large man had been more aware of the surroundings. Osgood's first instinct was to reach for his gun but he quickly thought better of it. Before he could react, the large man had let go of Joshua, turned, and begun running in the opposite direction. Joshua ran toward the lieutenant and nearly jumped into his arms. The lieutenant knew he had no choice but to hold his ground and take the punishment he knew was coming.

Officer Longley knew he had screwed up as soon as the large man had spotted his weapon. He also knew he had to do something to make up for his mistake. The big man was running fast and Longley wouldn't be able to catch him. He knew he wouldn't be able to bring that enormous man down by himself. He began to panic as he withdrew his Glock.

✻ ✻ ✻

Steve casually ate his popcorn while taking in the sights of the amusement park. He had always enjoyed parks because they represented an escape from work. To him, anything far removed from having to work for a living was a good thing. He could hang out in a park all day long, and to him, that was time well spent.

He had spotted the lieutenant standing at the entrance of the Ferris wheel and figured the action would start soon, and soon it did. A large man and a boy were approaching the lieutenant, but before they got within fifteen feet of him, another man approached from the shooting gallery. The large man suddenly let go of the young boy, turned, and began running straight in Steve's direction. Steve stood up and stepped out in front of him without thinking. The large man bowled into him and spun him around. At that moment, a shot rang out and Steve felt a sharp pain in his back. Suddenly he was having trouble breathing. The large man let go of Steve and Steve crumpled to the ground. As he took his last breath, Steve realized he didn't have to worry about work any longer.

Matthew didn't turn around to see what had happened to the man who stepped in front of him. He ran as fast as he could until he reached the backup car. The driver had seen Matthew coming at a run, so he had the car ready to go. Matthew jumped in and they were off before any pursuit was even considered.

Captain Jameson arrived at the Ferris wheel entrance just in time to see Officer Longley fire his weapon at the large man who had brought the lieutenant's son into the park. At first he thought the officer had missed hitting anyone but then he saw the informant drop to the ground as the large man again turned and ran.

"You idiot. You ruined the whole mission and you've shot an innocent man."

"I, uh, I'm sorry, sir."

"Just get back to the office. We'll clean this mess up and deal with you later."

"Yes, sir. I'm really, really sorry, sir."

Once the captain had determined that Steve was dead, he headed back to the lieutenant and his son.

"I guess you know what this means, Jaye," he said as he approached the lieutenant.

"Yes, sir. I do. I know you can't understand this since you don't have children, but I have to say, I'd do it over again for any of my children."

"You don't have to explain it to me, Jaye, but you will have to explain to the judge. Hopefully, for you, the judge will feel the same about his children. You realize you're going to have to go with us for now. We'll make sure Joshua gets home to Janet. You'll have a chance to talk to her later."

"Thank you, Mike," the lieutenant replied as the captain's phone rang.

30

JP AND EMILY WERE dressed as medical students. JP wore his normal short white coat, while Emily wore a similar coat with an emblem from a neighboring university. She was posing as a visiting medical student scheduled to do a six-week rotation at JP's hospital. She had the ID of a real student who was due to start a surgery rotation the following day. Emily even bore a slight resemblance to the woman she was pretending to be. JP was not sure how the Underground had obtained that information or the ID, but he was amazed at their resources.

The plan was straightforward. JP was giving the "visiting student" a tour of the hospital so she wouldn't feel lost when her rotation actually started. This would give them access to almost the whole hospital. The only challenge would be distracting the pharmacist long enough to find the chemotherapy drugs necessary for Katie's treatment. According to his grandfather, the Underground had never acquired drugs from the hospital pharmacy before, so JP doubted anyone would expect such a bold maneuver.

As JP and Emily approached the guard station at the front entrance of the hospital, JP snuck a glance at Emily. She looked much calmer than he felt. His pulse had to be running around one hundred and twenty beats per minute and with each one, he thought his heart was going to pound right out of his chest.

They neared the guard, who seemed totally bored with his job. He had hardly glanced at the IDs of the people who had entered before them and seemed much more interested in listening to his radio.

JP and Emily stopped in front of him and handed him their ID. The guard quickly returned JP's and started to hand Emily's back, but then took a second look.

"So, how long are you going to be here, Ms. Baldwin?"

Emily casually replied, "Six weeks, unless they keep me for bad behavior."

The guard half smiled, handed the card back, and JP and Emily walked into the hospital.

As they turned the corner out of sight of the guard, JP stopped and wiped his brow. "How do you stay so calm, Emily?"

"Who said I was calm? I've had years of practice hiding my emotions with my OCD. If I hadn't, I probably would have been terminated years ago."

JP and Emily made their way to the fourth-floor oncology ward of the hospital. JP often wondered why they even had an oncology ward, since very few cancers got treated now, under the guidelines of the Medical Reconciliation Act. He figured it was more for publicity than anything else, unless a few people had circumvented the Blumsfeld rule after all. At this point, though, he really couldn't have cared less why the unit was there. Despite the fact that he was a real medical student, he felt like a stranger in a foreign land. Still not comfortable in this new role he found himself in, he just wanted to get the drugs and get out. Life had been much simpler just a few days before.

He again glanced at Emily, who was still nonchalantly strolling along like she belonged there more than anyone else in the building. He couldn't but help admire her bravery and determination.

The pharmacy satellite serving the oncology floor was on the west corner of the floor. They expected only one pharmacist to be on duty, since very few patients actually occupied the various rooms on the floor. They approached the pharmacy door and waited until the arranged time to knock.

At the appointed time, JP and Emily knocked on the pharmacy door. Although the floor was minimally occupied, the pharmacist actually did seem to be busy and looked irritated at being interrupted.

"Can I help you?" he said.

"Hi, I'm a medical student here and I'm just showing one of our visiting students around the hospital. I thought it might be nice to have her see what our pharmacy satellites looked like. Do you have a couple of minutes to show her your work station?"

"Well, I am quite busy, but I guess I could..."

"Blue alert, oncology floor, Room 4-3-2," suddenly blared over the hospital intercom. JP glanced down the hall. A nurse with a puzzled look on her face was jumping out of her chair at the nurses' station. She was obviously agitated and confused.

The pharmacist stepped back into his satellite office and quickly began rolling the crash cart out the door, nearly running into JP and Emily.

"I'm sorry. Please get out of my way. The tour will have to wait. I have to go to this code NOW!" he said emphatically.

JP and Emily wasted no time. JP spotted the satellite's surveillance camera exactly where he had been told it would be located. He maneuvered through the small room and covered the lens with a piece of tape. He hoped no one was watching the monitor live, or he and Emily could be stopped before they came anywhere close to getting out of the hospital. But more than likely it was just a recording monitor to be reviewed if necessary.

They located the drugs in one of the cabinets and Emily quickly placed them in her backpack. Once she was back out of view, JP removed the tape from the surveillance camera and maneuvered out of the room without coming into camera range. Exiting the satellite, he saw the pharmacist come around the corner pushing the crash cart in front of him. He was obviously perturbed and mumbling to himself.

JP said, "That was a quick code. Did everything turn out okay?"

"It must have been a prank. There's not even a Room 432 on this floor. Everyone was running around checking all the rooms. The few patients we have up here are VIPs, of course, so everyone was quite nervous. But all were well, except for being upset about being disturbed. Heaven forbid that we were just trying to make sure they were okay. Anyway, where were we? Oh, yeah. You wanted a quick tour of the satellite. There's really not much to see, just a few cabinets and my computer and a few odds and ends."

"Well," JP improvised, "her university hospital uses only a centralized pharmacy. I just wanted her to see what a satellite was and how it could function more directly."

The pharmacist pushed his cart back into its storage area as he said, "Here it is. It works. What more can I say? For the most part, up here it's boring as hell."

"Thanks for your time. Have a nice afternoon," Emily chimed in. "Hopefully your day will get more exciting."

"Fat chance, but thanks."

Chatting as though they were on afternoon stroll in the park, Emily and JP casually headed toward the elevators. At the hospital entrance, the security guard was flirting with a young lady. They made a nonchalant exit.

31

EMILY AND JP ARRIVED back at his grandfather's house without incident. Their drug raid at the hospital had gone well. It had seemed almost too easy. Dr. Patrick was waiting anxiously on his front porch, pacing back and forth.

"We come bearing gifts, Grandpa. Everything went well. The timing of the fake code worked perfectly. Everyone on the floor was confused just long enough for us to get what we need. By the way, how did you pull that off? I thought a code could only be called from certain phones in the hospital."

"One of these days, I'll let you in on the little secret, but for now, the less you know, the better. Let's go in and get those drugs put away." Dr. Patrick opened the front door just as a second car pulled into the driveway.

At first, JP thought he and Emily had been followed, but he soon recognized the hulking figure of Matthew. As the big man got out of the car, JP noticed he did not have the usual lighthearted look on his face. Matthew followed them into the house without saying a word.

"Are you okay, Matthew?" Dr. Patrick asked as they walked into the living room. "You look shook up."

"The drop started out fine, but it was a setup. The MEU was waiting for us. I don't think the lieutenant was in on it though. He looked surprised when they moved in on us. I did get Joshua back to him, but then I had to turn and high tail it out of there. I can't say for sure, but it looked like they were handcuffing the lieutenant."

"That's too bad. I think he's a good man and a caring father. Otherwise he wouldn't have taken such a risk to get his daughter to us in the first place."

Matthew continued. "Unfortunately, that's not the only bad part. As I was running away, another man stepped in front of me. I couldn't tell if he did it on purpose to try and stop me or if he just turned at the wrong time. At any rate, as I ran into him we spun around, just as one of the officers shot at me. The other man took the bullet in his back, and I think it may have been fatal. I didn't have time to stick around and check."

Dr. Patrick put his hands up to his face and rubbed his eyes. "Do you have any idea if he was one of the unit guys or just an innocent bystander?"

"No, sir. I really didn't even get a good look at him since it happened so fast."

"Well this could cause them to intensify their investigation, either way. There's nothing we can do about it at this time. I just hope they're not too hard on the lieutenant. Hopefully they'll give him some leniency since he's on the Unit."

"How did JP and Emily do?" Matthew queried.

Before his grandfather could answer, JP responded with a little pride. "Our raid couldn't have gone better."

"That's good for little Katie," said Matthew. "How soon will she get started on her therapy?"

"I'll place a call to Dr. Jonason now and hopefully he'll be able to start it tomorrow. For your part Matthew, I would probably lay low for a while. I'm sure they will pass your description around to the city police. Heaven knows, you do stand out in a crowd."

"I will, Dr. Patrick. I think I'll be working out of the home for the next couple weeks."

The doctor looked over at JP and Emily. "As for you two," he said, "you did a great thing for Katie. Why don't you guys go out for dinner on me?"

"Thanks, Grandpa. Can you join us?"

Now it was time for Dr. Patrick to give others the exact details of the afternoon drop-off. "No. I've got some phone calls to make. You two have fun."

32

CAPTAIN JAMESON WAS TIRED. The adrenaline from the afternoon's events had worn off and now the shit was hitting the fan. He had been back at the office for several hours and had made little progress in figuring out how the day had gone south. He had also been informed of a drug theft at the hospital.

As soon as he arrived back, he had called the Minister of Health. Needless to say, the minister was not pleased that an innocent bystander had been killed during the mission. The captain knew if it had not been the street informant, things would have been much worse. However, it was still a negative mark on his career record.

He had spent the last two hours interrogating the lieutenant. Unfortunately, Jaye Osgood was proving to be nothing more than a father trying to help his children. He thus far had volunteered nothing useful about the Underground. His rendezvous had been arranged through the informant each time, and he apparently could provide no information about the identity or location of any of the local major players. The lieutenant's son, Joshua, had also proven to be a dead end. He had no idea where he had been kept the last couple weeks. All he would say was that the people were really nice and friendly and had taken good care of him.

All in all, the day had been a disaster, and he still had to deal with the theft of drugs from the oncology floor at the hospital. The pharmacist had reported nothing unusual during his shift other than the false alarm of a code on the floor. Either the pharmacist was lying or he was forgetting something. Perhaps letting the pharmacist sit in a cell overnight would jar his memory. The captain was too tired to deal with it tonight and he still had to run Joshua home. Although he had not been particularly close to Jaye and Janet, he thought he at least owed them the courtesy of driving Joshua home personally. In addition, the lieutenant had told him that his wife had known nothing about his dealings with the Underground. Although the captain found that somewhat difficult to believe, if it were true, he would have to fill her in on the situation. He wasn't looking forward to that task at all.

He gave the orders to keep the pharmacist overnight and then called Sam to let her know he would be late for their scheduled dinner plans. He then picked up Joshua and headed out of the Ministry of Health.

On the drive to the lieutenant's home, Joshua was rather sullen. He couldn't understand why his father wasn't taking him home.

"Captain. Is my father a bad person?"

Captain Jameson was startled by the question, both because they had ridden in silence most of the way and because he was at a loss as to what to say to the boy.

"Well, Joshua, by interacting with the Medical Underground, he broke the law. Yet that doesn't make him a bad person." He looked over at Joshua hoping his answer had placated the child. Joshua had a puzzled look on his face. "Do you understand that,

Joshua?"

Joshua looked out the window momentarily. "Actually, sir, I meant is he a bad person because he's part of the Medical Enforcement Unit?"

At a loss for an answer, the captain stared straight ahead. He was relieved when the Osgood home came into view and quickly changed the subject. "Joshua, I'm not sure your mom knows what happened today so I'm coming in with you for a while." He pulled into the drive and he and Joshua headed for the front door in silence.

33

IT HAD BEEN TWO weeks since JP and Emily had procured the drugs necessary for Katie's treatment. JP was on his way to pick Emily up at St. Francis of Assisi Church for dinner. JP hoped to get a chance to see Katie also. He had heard from Emily that the little girl was responding well to her treatments and had a good chance for a complete cure. He had bought her a teddy bear with little rabbit slippers on its paws and he wanted to give it to her himself.

When he walked down the stairs from the church to the safe house, Willy jumped out and said, "Boo!" and then started laughing as JP jumped. "I got you, JP."

JP laughed too. "You sure did, Willy. How ya doing, big guy?"

"I'm doing okay, JP. Where's Dr. John? Is he coming too?"

"No, no, Willy. I came by to pick up Emily, and of course to see you."

Willy smiled. He and JP had become friends, and Willy liked it that JP came over frequently.

"Hey, Willy. How's our little patient doing? Are you taking

good care of her?"

"You bet, JP. She doing real well. Dr. John says she getting much better. You want to see her?"

"Sure. I thought this little teddy bear might make her feel better. What do ya think?"

Willy smiled again. "You betcha, JP. Let's take it to her," he said quickly as he headed down the hall to Katie's room. They knocked and walked in.

JP was stunned by Katie's appearance, but made sure he acted normally. She was pale and her hair had thinned out, but she sat up in bed and smiled as they approached her bed.

"Hey, Katie. How's our favorite little patient doing?"

"I'm okay, but I wish Joshua was still here."

"I know, but I brought you someone to keep you company." He held out the teddy bear and the smile returned to her pretty face.

"Thanks, JP," she said taking the teddy bear and sitting it next to her in bed. "It's funny. It has bunnies on its feet. I think I'll call him Bunny Bear."

"That's a great name, Katie. I can see he likes it, too. What do you think Willy?"

"Good name. Katie a smart girl."

"You know it Willy."

Emily walked in "Hey, what's going on in here? Did someone throw a party and forget to invite me?"

"Hi, Emily. I just wanted to see how our star patient was doing," JP replied.

"He brought me a teddy bear," Katie said with a big smile on her face as she held it up to show Emily. "His name is Bunny Bear."

"Why, he's very cute, Katie. I hope he didn't eat those poor little bunnies before he turned them into slippers. "

"Noooo," Katie said laughing.

"Well, I hate to break up this little party, but Grandpa is expecting us for dinner and we're running a little late. Willy, you keep taking good care of Katie."

"I will, JP," Willy added a salute to his affirmation.

JP and Emily left Katie's room and headed up the stairs. As they entered the sacristy, Father Mark met them. "Hi, guys. How is everything with our little patient?"

"Excellent. Willy has everything under control. By the way, we're heading over to Grandpa's to help plan Willy's surprise party. Any good ideas for a theme?"

"Oh, I'm sure your grandpa will have plenty of them. I'll see you guys Sunday if not before. You tell that old man hi for me," Father Mark added, as he headed down the stairs to check on Katie and Willy.

Emily and JP left the church and headed over to Dr. Patrick's house. They were looking forward to dinner with him. His cooking was always a gourmet treat. The drive was not long, but both were quiet until Emily broke the silence. "That was really nice of you to bring Katie that teddy bear, JP."

"It wasn't much. She's a great little girl and I'm happy she's doing so well."

"Well, it was still a nice gesture."

JP smiled and concentrated on his driving. He really wanted to just stare at Emily because he was definitely falling in love, although he wasn't quite ready to let on about it. This was new territory for him. As he pulled into his grandpa's drive, he thought what a tragedy it would have been if this beautiful person sitting next to him had been terminated. A chill went down his spine.

34

TWO WEEKS HAD GONE by and there still had been little progress made on either the lieutenant's case or the theft of the drugs from the oncology pharmacy. The lieutenant remained in confinement at the Ministry of Health building, but had provided no useful information that might lead to further arrests of the Underground. Over the objections of the lieutenant's wife, his son Joshua had also been interrogated several more times as well. But again, he had been unable to provide any useful information about where he had been held during his confinement.

The video from the pharmacy satellite had also been a dead end. The criminals that had taken the drugs had been smart enough to block the camera prior to entering the room. The only additional information the pharmacist had remembered was the fact that a medical student had brought a visiting student by to see how a pharmacy worked. Unfortunately he could not remember their names and couldn't even give much of a description other than it was a young man and a young woman. He did recall that the prank blue alert code had occurred while the two students were on the floor. Captain Jameson knew that was no coincidence—but he had yet to prove anything. To make matters worse, the Minister of Health was catching heat for the botched police work, which had resulted in a dead informant, Underground escapees and a drug heist at a hospital pharmacy.

About the only thing Captain Jameson had accomplished was suspending the rookie officer who botched the raid and then shot the informant. The captain was so furious—and embarrassed—that he was pressing for Officer Longley to be criminally charged. Longley might well prove to be a scapegoat, but Captain Jameson knew that he would ultimately be held accountable for the actions of his officers. His ears were still ringing from the admonishment he received from his boss, Dr. Atherton.

"Mike, I know police work can be complicated. And I understand one of your officers is largely to blame for the incident at the park. But you hired the man and you direct the unit's work. The failure to resolve this case—and to prevent it in the first place—reflects very poorly on your performance and leadership. We're in quite a hole here, captain, one that we need to crawl out of quickly or be buried in. Do you understand?"

"Yes, sir. Unfortunately, I hear you loud and clear."

Dr. Atherton didn't mention his daughter. But Captain Jameson felt that if his career crumbled, so would his relationship with Sam.

Prior to the events of the last couple of weeks, he had seriously considered asking Sam to move in with him, but now he was not so sure. Sam had told him repeatedly that her father greatly respected him and that she didn't think he had a problem with their relationship. The captain's phone rang.

"Jameson," he answered tersely.

"Uh, is this a bad time?" Sam questioned.

"Oh, Sam. No, I was just deep in thought, going over the lieutenant's case and the pharmacy theft case. We're kind of running into dead ends on both. I'm afraid your dad's not too pleased with me at the present time."

"Mike, you know he has a lot of respect for you and knows you're doing everything you can."

"Well, I hope so. But he blasted me pretty good, and, frankly, I can't blame him. So what's up?"

"I guess you forgot about our dinner plans."

"I'm so sorry, Sam. These cases have me all screwed up. I was planning on watching the video of the hospital entrance from the night of the theft to see if I could pick out anything new. You mind if I take a rain check?"

Sam laughed. "I'll tell you what. You bring the video home and I'll make you dinner. We can watch it together. After all, what girl can resist a dinner and a movie?"

"Sounds like a good plan to me. I don't think I would be good company otherwise."

"Then it's a date. I'll be over around seven. Don't start the movie without me."

"Don't worry. I wouldn't want you to miss the best part," the captain said as he laughed and hung up the phone. He was always amazed at how Sam could make him feel better even when he was just talking to her on the phone. He really didn't want this young lady to get away from him.

35

JP AND EMILY WERE having fun planning Willy's surprise birthday party. It was going to be held at Dr. Patrick's house so they could easily decorate and get everything ready without Willy finding out. The guest list was obviously limited. Only those who were involved in some way with the Underground knew of Willy's existence and most of them had actually met Willy at some time or another at the safe house.

Willy was a very big fan of golf. He watched all the various tournaments on television and kept track of his favorite players. No one quite understood how or why Willy was so fascinated by it. The various members of the Underground would often visit the safe house and watch golf with him. Most were amazed at the details that Willy could rattle off about the various tour players as well as the history of golf.

It had therefore been an easy decision to come up with a theme for the party. The required attire for those invited would be golf outfits and Dr. Patrick's house would be transformed as much as possible into an indoor golf course. Dr. Patrick had even obtained a virtual-reality hitting screen from one of his past associates. Willy, for the first time ever, would actually get to hit a real golf ball with a real golf club.

"JP, have you picked out your outfit for the party yet?" Emily asked sweetly.

"Well, I've heard one of Willy's all-time favorite players was Payne Stewart. I know that before he died in a plane crash, Payne Stewart always wore knickers on the course. He was apparently not only a good golfer, but also a good Christian man and father. I don't know if Willy liked him for that or not, but it makes me wonder. At any rate, I've decided to wear knickers in his honor. I'm sure Willy will approve. What about you, Emily? Are you going to wear one of those nice little skorts the young ladies wear on tour?"

"I'm not even sure I know what a skort is, but it sounds like something you'd like me to wear."

JP turned a little red. "I didn't mean anything bad by that," he said. "But I do think you'd look good in one."

Emily blushed a little too and quickly changed the subject. "Is Katie still responding to treatment well?"

"Grandpa says she's doing great. Dr. Jonason thinks that from the way she's responding, she probably has a great chance of a complete cure. Unfortunately, even if she's cured, she may not be able to go back to her parents since she's now in the system as having been referred to the End of Life Care Center. Not only that, but apparently her father, the lieutenant from the MEU, is still being held. He is probably going to be charged with circum-venting the Act, all because he tried to help his little girl."

"I wish we could do something for him."

"Well, I'm sure helping save his little girl has made him happy. After all, he was willing to sacrifice himself for her. Unfortunately, I don't think there's anything else we can do."

"Do you think Katie will feel well enough to come to the party for Willy? I'm sure he would like that, since they've become such good friends."

"Hopefully she can. It will probably be up to Dr. Jonason. If Katie has her way, I know she wouldn't miss it for the world."

JP was thrilled that Katie now had a second chance at life. Still, in the back of his mind, he couldn't help feeling concerned about how happy the life of this child could be as a fugitive of the law. Regardless, he knew at that moment that being a doctor was what he was meant to do and he would never let anyone go without proper medical care.

36

SAM ARRIVED AT CAPTAIN Jameson's house on time and walked right inside. She heard the captain taking a shower so she headed to the kitchen with her bag of groceries, to start dinner. She felt quite at home at Jameson's place and wondered why he hadn't asked her to move in with him. She was pretty sure the fact that her father was his boss had something to do with it. She hoped she could allay his concerns, because she was ready to make the big move.

As Sam was preparing the salad, Captain Jameson walked into the kitchen and gave her a big hug from behind. "I thought something smelled good when I stepped out of the shower."

"I haven't started cooking yet, Mike."

"I was talking about you, my dear."

"Oh, you really know how to sweet-talk a girl."

"Not any girl, just you."

"That sounds even better."

"What's for dinner?"

"Why don't you just go get the video ready and I'll surprise you."

"I hope you're ready to be bored to death."

"Hopefully my snoring won't bother you too much."

Captain Jameson laughed as he left the kitchen and headed toward his living room.

"Have you got the movie all primed?" Sam said as she brought dinner into the living room.

"You bet. Ooh! That smells good."

"I hope you like it."

The captain started the surveillance video and he and Sam began eating. The video droned on and both enjoyed the stir-fry that Sam had prepared. After they had finished, Sam carried the dishes into the kitchen and then returned and sat on the couch next to the captain. She was close to falling asleep when she suddenly sat up and asked the captain to rewind the video.

"What? Did you see something deserving of an Oscar?"

"No, no. I think I recognized someone."

"Well it is from the hospital where you work."

"I know, but I think I saw JP and his girlfriend."

"What's unusual about that? He does work there."

"I know. But she doesn't, and I think she was wearing a med student coat."

"Maybe she was just cold and borrowed one of his coats."

"That could be true, but it looked like she was showing the guard a medical student ID."

The captain rewound the video and they both watched with more attention as JP and his girlfriend entered the hospital. Just as Sam had noticed, JP's girlfriend did indeed show the guard an ID that looked like a medical student ID. The captain rewound the video again and took note of the time the couple entered the hospital as well as the guard that had checked them through. He also made a mental note to have the pharmacist watch the video to see if he could possibly identify JP and his girlfriend. It was a long shot, but at this point, he needed any break in the case.

"Just how well do you know JP, Sam?"

"Before I met you, we used to study together and sit together in class all the time. He's a terrific guy and really smart. I actually thought we would start dating at one point, but he seemed pretty shy. He did invite me over to his grandfather's house once, but I was unable to go. It's hard to believe he would be involved in any nefarious activities."

"Did you ever end up meeting his grandfather or did he ever tell you anything about him?"

"No I never did get to meet him, but I do know he lives in town and is quite a man, according to JP."

"I might need to look into him. Does anything else strike you as odd about this video, Sam?"

"No, not really. Except that every time I see JP's girlfriend, it seems as though I've seen her before. But I just can't put my finger on it."

"Keep thinking about it. It might come to you. I'm so glad you're here. I never would have picked up on JP and his girlfriend. Do you mind watching the rest of it with me? Two sets of eyes are obviously better than one."

"I don't mind at all. In fact, I brought ingredients to make a delicious breakfast. I hope you don't think that's being too forward of me."

"Not at all. That's by far the best offer for breakfast I've ever had."

Sam smiled and snuggled next to him. It was going to be a good night.

37

JP WAS ON HIS way over to his grandfather's. The party for Willy was only a week away and there was a lot to do to get the house ready. Emily was meeting him there, along with Matthew and Father Mark. JP marveled at how many people were involved in throwing a party for someone whom society would have discarded long ago. Willy had obviously touched the lives of numerous people at the safe house, and most would lay down their lives for him.

As he drove, JP thought back at how his life had changed in the last couple of months. He had left his safe, secure world as a medical student and stepped into a world of secret hideouts, stealth missions, and people whom he never would have thought he ever would meet. How things could quickly change. Already, he couldn't imagine his life without Emily. He truly hoped she felt the same way. He thought back to the first time he had seen her in front of the class. How could anyone parade such a beautiful person in front of a class like that, let alone terminate her just because of an illness? No, there was no use denying it—he had truly found a calling.

He was about halfway to his grandfather's house when he noticed a car that seemed to be tailing him. He decided to make a couple extra turns just to make sure. The car followed him the first block, but didn't make the second turn so JP relaxed a little and drove on. He wondered if he was becoming paranoid or if he was just becoming more aware. He continued on and soon arrived, failing to notice another car that slowly pulled by while snapping photographs of both JP and the house.

JP walked in and found the rest of the group already working on the decorations. He was amazed at the transformation of the house already. There were posters of many current PGA tour players already hung on the wall and part of the virtual hitting area had been assembled. JP walked over to Emily and gave her a one-armed hug. She smiled and warmly accepted it.

"It looks like you guys started without me."

"Actually, your grandfather has done most of this so far. We just got here a little before you. I think he could actually do all this without us."

"I wouldn't doubt it. He never ceases to amaze me," JP replied. He walked over and shook Matthew's large hand. "Good to see you again. Where are Father Mark and Grampa?"

"They went out to get some sort of material to make a putting green. They should be back soon, I think."

"Cool. I can't wait to see Willy's face when he walks in here next week."

"That's for sure, JP. It's going to be a day to remember. I hope everyone can make it."

"I, for one, wouldn't miss it for the world," JP said as his grandfather and Father Mark came in through the garage entrance.

Dr. Patrick gave JP a little wink. "Hey JP. I'm glad you're here.

I want you and Emily to set up the putting green area."

"I'm sure we can handle that, Grandpa."

"We left the materials and the plans out in the garage. We'll keep things going in here."

JP and Emily headed out to the garage as Dr. Patrick leaned over to Father Mark and whispered, "You better get those wedding vows warmed up."

Father Mark laughed. "Doing a little scheming, are we?"

38

LIEUTENANT OSGOOD WAS DEPRESSED. He had been held at the Ministry of Health since his arrest. Joshua had been allowed to go home, but he had been brought back in several more times for questioning. Osgood was not happy about that, but there was nothing he could do about it. He had made his bed and now he had to sleep in it, even if it was a bed of nails.

Captain Jameson had questioned Osgood several more times. Each time he had given the same empty answers. Jameson had not been to see him for several days now, so the lieutenant figured he had finally realized that he knew nothing useful about the Underground.

Unfortunately, they had not allowed Osgood's wife to speak with him at all. He wondered how she and the other children were doing. He feared never seeing them again. He expected no sympathy, even though he had served in the Medical Enforcement Unit honorably for several years. That was the Blumsfeld rule. No exceptions; no special treatment. In fact, he might be treated more harshly, just to set an example to the others.

He wondered how Katie was doing. He had risked everything for his little girl and now again mulled over whether he had done the right thing. He had placed her in the hands of people he really knew nothing about and, in the process, had essentially given up his entire family. Was one life worth all that? The answer was obvious to him, but sitting alone in his jail cell put doubt into him. If only he could find out how she was faring, then he could have some peace of mind.

The cell door suddenly buzzed and the Minister of Health entered.

39

THE CAPTAIN SAT AT his computer doing some research on JP's background. His mood had improved significantly thanks to Sam. She had come up with the one lead that could help him bust the local Underground resistance. It seemed that Sam's friend JP was most likely involved in some kind of activities with the Underground and would hopefully be the key to finding its leaders and uncovering its activities in this region.

From the video, the guard at the front entrance of the hospital had definitely identified JP and his girlfriend as the two students who had come in on the day of the pharmacy theft. He clearly remembered JP introducing her as a visiting medical student. In addition, the pharmacist had also identified them as the two students who had visited the pharmacy satellite during the time the medications had been stolen. These two facts alone would justify bringing JP in for questioning, but the captain had bigger fish to fry than one young medical student. He wanted to bring down the entire resistance. If he could do that, there would be no limit to where his career could take him.

He had placed a tail on JP and was sure something would turn up sooner or later. In addition, although she felt uncomfortable about it, Sam was going to see if she could get any information from him. It was unlikely he would voluntarily give her any useful information since he knew of her relationship with the captain. Then again, he might just inadvertently let something useful slip out.

If Captain Jameson got the chance, he would also have JP's girlfriend followed. How she fit into all this was still unclear. She could just be a local resistance operative. However, Sam seemed sure she had seen her somewhere before and that could mean she played a different role. He hoped Sam would eventually remember where she had seen her. That could possibly open up another door.

Sam was coming over shortly and he wanted to get his work done before she arrived. He pulled up JP's family history and began reading. Both parents had been practicing physicians and neither had ever raised even a minor stir when it came to the Medical Reconciliation Act. His mother had died suddenly, but his father still practiced in another city. He noted that JP's grandfather had also been a physician who practiced before the Act took effect. He would probably be quite elderly now, and it seemed unlikely that he would have anything to do with the Underground.

Sam came in just as Jameson was about finished reading JP's dossier. He started to close the file when he noticed that JP's parents also had a daughter. He clicked on her file and suddenly he sat up and read more intensely. She had actually been JP's twin and had been terminated at an End of Life Care Center because of renal failure. He now had a motive for JP's probable involvement. He'd better check out JP's father as well. What better motive for him to be involved than the loss of his daughter?

Captain Jameson had recently seen what his own lieutenant

would do for his daughter. The squeaky clean record of JP's father might just be a cover for more covert activity.

"What ya doing?" Sam said as she bent over and gave the captain a kiss on the cheek.

"Just a little research on your friend JP. Did you know he had a twin sister?"

"He never mentioned anything to me about her. Where is she now?"

"She died when they were very young. She was actually terminated in the Care Center after she developed renal failure from something called post-strep *glo...mer...u-lo-neph-ritis* or something like that. It's interesting that he wouldn't have mentioned her at some point."

"He might not even know about her. I don't know about you, but I can't remember much about my own life till I was about three or four years old. How old was she when she was terminated?"

"It says here that she was just a little over two. I guess you could be right. If he does know about it, though, it could be just enough for him to oppose the Act and to get involved with the Underground."

"But that would be so disappointing. JP has been such a good friend and always struck me as a really great guy with a big heart."

"Maybe too big of a heart?" Captain Jameson said.

"I suppose so, but he still doesn't strike me as the rebel type. "

"Any more thoughts on where you might have seen his girlfriend?"

"No, but I still feel like I've met her somewhere."

40

NEARLY ALL THE PREPARATIONS for Willy's surprise party were completed. JP had a great time with Emily, putting together the putting green in the garage. The more time he spent with her, the more time he wanted to spend with her. He had never felt like that about anyone else. She still exhibited some of the signs of her OCD, but JP tried to act like he didn't notice them. The last thing he wanted was for her to feel embarrassed around him. He knew it must be hard for her and couldn't begin to imagine the inner pain she suffered.

Once they finished putting the final touches on the putting green, they went back into the house.

"Wow. This place looks great. Willy is going to love this."

"You know it, JP," his grandfather replied as he walked into the living room from the kitchen. "He's gonna think he done died and gone to Heaven."

"Well, I wouldn't go that far," Father Mark chimed in with a little laugh. "But I'm sure he's going to have the time of his life."

"How's the putting green coming along?"

"It's all done. Emily and I make a good team."

"Did you make sure he did everything right, Emily? He's not real mechanically inclined, you know."

"He did just fine, Dr. Patrick. I think he's a chip off the old block."

"The key word there is 'old,' I would say," JP added with a big smile on his face.

"Watch it, you little whippersnapper. I might have to take you down right here in front of everybody."

"That, I would pay to see," Matthew said as everyone laughed.

"Well, I hate to disappoint everyone, but I really need to get home and do some studying."

"Lame excuse if you ask me," his grandfather added as everyone laughed again. "I do need to discuss a few things with Father Mark and Matthew, though. JP, would you mind dropping Emily back off at St. Francis?"

"It would be my pleasure, Grandpa," JP replied and gave his grandfather a little wink.

Everyone said their goodbyes until the big party and then JP and Emily left in JP's car. He was so captivated with her, he failed to notice the car that pulled out of an alley and started following them.

※ ※ ※

Captain Jameson's cell phone rang as he and Sam were just sitting down for dinner. "This is Captain Jameson."

"Yes, sir. This is Officer England. I'm sorry to bother you, sir, but I'm on surveillance detail tonight, following the medical student named James Patrick. He spent the evening at a residence on Independence Street. I believe it belongs to his grandfather, a retired surgeon. What I'm calling about is the fact that he just left with a young woman meeting the description of the woman who went into the hospital with him on the day of the pharmacy theft. In report, we were told you also wanted her followed. I'm following them, but thought you might want to get another officer ready to do surveillance on her."

"That's great, Robert. Keep your surveillance at a distance. We don't want them getting suspicious. When they stop, contact your supervisor and he'll arrange her tail. You continue on Mr. Patrick. Good work. Keep me informed if there's anything else unusual. Otherwise, work through your supervisor."

The captain hung up his phone and smiled at Sam. "It seems we've caught up with JP's girlfriend. She just left his grandfather's house with JP. Now we'll find out where she lives and perhaps a little more about her. You recognizing her on that video may have been just what we needed to break this case. Have I told you that you are incredible?"

"Well, maybe once or twice, but a girl can never hear it enough," she said coyly.

41

DR. PATRICK WAS EXPECTING around forty or fifty guests for the party. Many more had wanted to come, but were unable to because of prior commitments. All in all, there would be people from all walks of life there to honor Willy.

His bones creaking, Dr. Patrick eased into a chair and sipped a little Scotch. He was getting old, and knew he would soon have to pass the torch to someone younger, to carry on the work of the Underground. The operation on little Joshua had made that obvious to him. Now that the Act had been in effect for over thirty years, he doubted whether it could ever be overturned. Most people had just accepted it as the way it had to be and the resistance seemed to be lessening. He prayed something would change to wake people up. He could only continue his small role.

✳ ✳ ✳

It had been a hard week at the hospital, but today was Willy's party and JP could not wait to get to his grandfather's house. He had been unable to spend any time with Emily, making his time at work drag even more. That would change today. He had planned to pick her up, but she had called and said she was riding over with Father Mark, Willy, and little Katie.

Katie had continued to respond to the chemotherapy, so much so that Dr. Jonason had given her permission to go to the party. It would be her first time out of the safe house at St. Francis since her arrival. Emily thought it would be better if she rode along with her. JP agreed and planned to meet them at the party.

He left his apartment and pulled out into traffic. A gray sedan pulled out behind him.

❋ ❋ ❋

Captain Jameson was enjoying the weekend. The past week had been busy with the usual routine business, but also with the ongoing investigation of the drug theft and the Underground. Sam had also had a busy week at the hospital, so both were happy to finally have some time together.

"Do you have to go in at all today, Mike?"

"Nope. Today I'm all yours."

"That's terrific."

"How about you? Any studying you have to do?"

"As a matter of fact, you're my only lesson."

"What do you say about a trip out to the lake for a little cruise on my boat?" the captain asked as he gave her a hug and a kiss on the forehead.

"That sounds like fun. I didn't know you owned a boat."

"It's nothing fancy, but being out on the water relaxes me."

"Well, I want you nice and relaxed this weekend so let's go for it."

"Okay. Let's put together some food and drink and...." His

cell phone began to ring. "Jameson."

"This is England, sir. I've got Mr. Patrick's surveillance duty today. He left his apartment earlier and has again returned to his grandfather's house."

"Why does that deserve an interruption of my day?" Captain Jameson replied somewhat tersely.

"There seems to be a large gathering at his grandfather's house. There are numerous vehicles parked around the location and just since I've been observing the house, I've seen at least six or seven people enter the residence."

"Did you see anything else that makes you think there's something of interest going on? Sounds pretty innocuous to me."

"Sir, I thought it might be enough to take a closer look."

"It could just be a cookout or something. I don't think we're going to be busting any doors down without more to go on, but let me know if you see anything more conclusive."

"Yes, sir." England replied somewhat sheepishly and hung up.

"What happened, Mike?"

"Oh, our tail on JP is just getting a little antsy. JP's grandfather is having a get-together and my guy seems to think it's time to move in. More than likely he's just getting tired of his assignment."

"Now that you brought up the subject of JP, how long are you going to keep surveillance on him? Don't you think you would have caught him doing something by now?"

"There's no set time, but as long as he's a person of interest and I have the resources, we'll keep watching him. Besides, we do have good evidence he was the one who stole the drugs from the pharmacy at the hospital. Now enough shop talk. Let's get back to planning some relaxation."

"Okay, but I feel awful for JP. He's been a good friend and I'd hate to see anything bad happen to him."

"If he's not involved in anything illegal, then nothing is going to happen to him. Maybe he was just trying to impress his girl-friend by showing her around the hospital, but it still is suspicious enough to warrant surveillance. Now let's forget about JP and have some fun."

❋ ❋ ❋

JP arrived well ahead of the guest of honor and went into his grandfather's house. Many of the other guests had already arrived and the party was in full swing. He recognized a few of them from his visits to the safe house and from meetings at his grandpa's house. For the most part, though, the other guests were strangers. Interestingly, there were people of all ages, in-cluding several fairly young children. JP didn't know who was involved with the Underground and who had been the recipient of the Underground's activities. The good news was that he had the whole evening to mix and mingle and hear the stories of the various guests.

❋ ❋ ❋

Sam and the captain finished loading his truck for their trip to the lake and headed off. The lake was located about twenty minutes outside of town so they would be there within half an hour. The sun was shining and the sky was cloudless; a perfect setting for a romantic evening cruise.

The captain's boat was docked at a marina, in a covered bay. He and Sam removed the boat cover, lowered the boat into the water with the lift, and were quickly heading out of the marina.

The captain opened a bottle of wine as he slowly guided the boat away from the dock. Sam opened a container of various types of cheeses and both sat back and breathed in the fresh air. They were about a quarter mile from the marina when the captain's cellphone rang.

"Jameson! What is it?" he practically yelled.

"Yes, sir. Sorry to bother you. This is Officer McNeely. I've been on surveillance of the young lady at St. Francis Catholic Church this evening. She and three others left the church a short time ago. One was a priest, one was an adult male, and the other was a little girl. I've followed them to the same house where England first picked up her tail last week. It seems they're having a big gathering."

"Yes, I know. England already notified that Mr. Patrick had shown up there as well. I'm sure he's watching the house like you. Is there anything to suggest that it's more than just a friendly get-together or cookout?"

"Uhhh. No, sir. I guess not. The only unusual thing was that I could have sworn that the adult that accompanied the priest and the young lady was mentally challenged."

"What do you mean by that?"

"I think it was someone with Down's syndrome. I mean I haven't seen one of those in a long time, but from a distance it kinda looked like one."

"I'm sure you were mistaken."

"You're probably right, sir. I was pretty far off. But he did look different."

"Okay. See if you can meet up with England and continue your surveillance."

"Yes, sir."

Sam was spreading cheese on a cracker. "What was that all about, Mike?"

"Oh, more of the same. We have another man watching JP's girlfriend. Apparently, she and three others showed up at the same gathering as JP. Now where were we? Oh yeah. I'm supposed to be relaxing. Maybe I should pitch this phone into the lake. Better yet, hand me that bottle of wine."

"Perhaps your men are on to something."

"Not you too."

"Well, I know I said I can't imagine JP being involved in all of this, but I do remember sitting in class with him earlier this year when he mentioned feeling sorry for a girl that was being presented to the class. She was going to be terminated. He seemed quite upset about how the professor was treating her. It seemed strange coming from him at the time." Sam put the cracker down untasted. "Wait a minute! I just realized why JP's girlfriend looked familiar to me. She looks just like that girl with the OCD. That's not possible, is it, Mike?"

The captain put the cork back in the wine bottle and sighed. "I guess I'm not going to get any relaxation. Are you sure?"

"I'm fairly positive. She looked familiar from the first time JP introduced her to us, but I couldn't put my finger on it. I think her hair is different, but I would put money on it that she is the girl with OCD. "

The captain sighed again and poured his glass of wine into the lake. "We don't publicize when patients are taken from the End of Life Care Center by the Underground, but there was a young lady taken several months ago while she was being transported over from the hospital. We never found her and we're sure the Underground was behind it. Now whether JP's girlfriend is that girl I don't know, but my interest in this party they're attending has just gone up. You're absolutely positive she looks like the girl you saw in class with JP?"

"I'm almost certain."

"I need you to be pretty damn positive if we're going to burst into their little get-together tonight."

Sam stared out into the water and thought for a couple of

minutes. "Look, I can't say one hundred percent that she's the same girl, but I know I've seen her before. It all makes sense with JP and his possible involvement with the Underground."

The captain thought for a couple minutes and then pulled out his cell phone. "McNeely, this is Jameson. Is the gathering still going on at the house?"

"Yes, sir. I've met up with England and we've been watching it since we talked to you."

"Okay. Stay put. I'm going to have our team pay them a little visit. Call me if the situation changes. I'll let you know when the team's on the way."

"Yes, sir. We'll be here."

Jameson turned the boat around and headed back to the marina. He then made two additional calls; one to his team leader and one to the Minister of Health, to update him. Finishing the call, he turned to Sam.

"Well, here's your chance to see what we do, Sam. Are you up for it?"

"I wouldn't miss it."

※ ※ ※

The last of the guests arrived just before the guest of honor was expected. JP was anxious for Willy to get there, but was also happy that Emily would soon be there as well. He was looking forward to spending the evening with her. He had begun to feel empty unless she was around. He wasn't sure what that meant, but he hoped she felt the same way.

JP mingled with the guests and heard many stories of heroism, as well as many stories from grateful people who had been touched by the safe house in one way or another. He watched his grandfather making the rounds doing what he did best, making everyone feel at home. He was also introduced to Willy's parents, which made him realize even more the serious nature of the Underground.

His grandfather's phone rang and Dr. Patrick whistled to get everyone's attention. After a brief moment, the guests quieted down and turned toward him.

"That was Father Mark. They're just about a block away so everyone get ready for the surprise." He turned down the lights and everyone remained quiet except for an occasional whisper or two. One minute later, they heard car doors closing and all fell silent.

Willy walked through the front door and the lights were turned on. "Surprise!" everyone yelled in unison. Willy at first didn't realize what was going on, but then everyone started saying, "Happy Birthday."

Willy smiled broadly and started mingling and giving almost everyone hugs. Then JP spotted Emily as she came through the door and he casually headed over to her. She looked beautiful to him as always. Little Katie was staying close to Emily with Bunny Bear held tightly in her arms.

"Well, I think we pulled off the surprise."

"You're telling me, JP. He didn't have any idea about it on his way over. What do you think, Katie? Do you think we surprised Willy?"

"Yeah. He looks really happy."

"I'm sure he's going to have a great time."

"Can I get you two something to eat or drink?" JP asked.

"What do ya think, Katie? Ready to join the party?"

"Yeah. I'd like some cake."

"Cake coming right up," JP said as he headed to the kitchen.

✳ ✳ ✳

Lieutenant Osgood was sitting in his cell thinking back to better times, when an officer came in and said he was being transferred to another facility.

"Am I staying in town?" he asked, not expecting an honest answer.

"I don't know, Lieutenant. I was just instructed to escort you out to a waiting vehicle."

"What about my belongings?"

"I'm sure they will be sent along after you."

The lieutenant eyed the officer skeptically, but knew he was not in a bargaining position. He stood up and exited the cell with the officer.

The lieutenant was led from the Ministry of Health to a waiting SUV with shaded windows. He was placed alone in the back seat. A glass screen separated him from the driver and front passenger seat. The screen was tinted enough to prevent the lieutenant from seeing who was sitting on the other side. After several minutes, the back door opened again and Osgood's wife, Janet, and Dr. Atherton stepped in. Osgood's reunion with his wife was short-lived before the car started moving.

As they drove through the city, Lieutenant Osgood began to wonder if perhaps his wife was now also in trouble. Why else would Janet be here with him? She had not been allowed to see him since his arrest so her presence did not bode well. However, he could not understand why they were in the car together. If she indeed had been arrested earlier without his knowledge, surely they would not be transported to another facility together. He became worried about their children. If he and Janet were both arrested, their kids would essentially become orphans. His mood, which had been momentarily lifted by seeing Janet, suddenly became sullen. The minister remained quiet and the lieutenant believed he was in no position to question him.

✻ ✻ ✻

Captain Jameson briefed his team on the target house. A floor plan had been obtained from the county records and his men at the scene had sent digital photos of the house back to him. The entry team would consist of nine men. They would enter the door on "white," the term for the front of the house. A second security team would surround the house and watch for anyone trying to escape on "black" while snipers watched the various windows for any sign of resistance. Once the house and its occupants were secure, the captain would enter and be briefed on those present and their status.

"Their past history would probably negate any armed resistance, but be on your toes. Use the normal rules of engagement before using any lethal force, but do remember you have the right to defend yourself. Remember our men on site have noted some children present. Lastly, this is a picture of a young woman who was kidnapped from the End of Life Care Center a few months ago. We have reason to believe she may be one of those at the gathering. Any questions?"

"Our intel reports as many as thirty to forty occupants, are we to assume they are all targets?"

"As always, consider them all potential Underground operatives. We will sort them out once the scene is secure. Are there any other questions?" The men shook their heads. "Okay, then, let's roll."

The team filed out of the briefing room and entered two armored vehicles. Captain Jameson stepped into the lead vehicle and Sam stepped in beside him. On seeing this, the driver looked over and said, "Sir?"

"She's with me."

Sam couldn't believe she was actually riding in an armored

vehicle with the enforcement unit's elite team, on their way to a raid. Earlier in her life, music had brought this kind of excitement to her, but nothing in medical school had come close. It did trouble her that JP was involved in all this, but if he had gone against the Medical Reconciliation Act, he would have to pay the price. She had no control over that and didn't feel any guilt about it. She felt a sense of power as the trucks made their way through the streets, on their way to their target. She looked back over her shoulder, scanning the members of the entry team.

All wore Kevlar vests and helmets and carried assault rifles. She could tell the adrenalin was flowing in the men. They reminded her of large tigers waiting to pounce on their victims. She understood much better why the captain thoroughly enjoyed his job.

The two vehicles approached the neighborhood of their target house and she saw the men getting more focused. The chatter stopped and everyone seemed to be going over the planned entry in his mind. The captain leaned over to her and said, "When we pull up to a stop, the men will exit the vehicles quickly and quietly and take up their positions. I'll move up to the house with the team and go in once the situation is secure. You'll have to stay in the vehicle or at least out in the street. I don't want anything to happen to you, especially since your father doesn't know you're here."

"Aye, aye, Captain! I wish I could join you." Sam replied with a little pout on her face.

❋ ❋ ❋

Willy was having the time of his life. He seemed uninterested in the food and drink. He was enthralled with the various posters and golf paraphernalia all around the living room. He finally made his way to the virtual reality hitting area and his eyes lit up.

"It's your turn to play, Willy." Dr. Patrick said as Willy lifted up one of the balls on the mat in front of the screen. "The picture you see on the screen is the—"

"First hole, Pebble Beach." Willy blurted out excitedly.

"You're right, Willy. You can play the whole course right here."

"Real cool, Dr. John." Willy said as he picked up a driver. He placed a ball on the rubber tee, stood up with more intensity than Dr. Patrick expected, and took a swing. The ball struck the screen and then the virtual reality showed it flying thru the air on Pebble Beach's number one hole. Thrilled, Willy looked over at Dr. Patrick with a smile that was worth a million dollars.

※ ※ ※

The lieutenant looked at the Minister of Health with a quizzical look on his face, but Dr. Atherton just stared forward without saying a word. Osgood then looked over at Janet, who shrugged her shoulders and shook her head. She clearly didn't know why she was there.

The lieutenant also wondered why he was not handcuffed and why there were no armed guards in the back with them. He assumed the minister must not consider him a flight risk although the thought of flight had crossed his mind.

※ ※ ※

Willy was thoroughly enjoying himself with the virtual golf. He had played nearly all the holes at Pebble Beach and showed no signs of slowing down. Only when the birthday cake was brought out from the kitchen with forty burning candles was Dr. Patrick finally able to draw his attention away from the screen.

As Willy approached the large birthday cake, everyone began

singing "Happy Birthday" again. He sang along with everyone. When the song was over, Dr. Patrick said, "Make a wish, Willy, and then blow out the candles."

Willy replied, "That's a lot of candles, Dr. John," and everyone broke out in a laugh. With one large breath, Willy proceeded to extinguish all the candles. Claps were heard around the room and Willy grinned from ear to ear.

"Okay, Willy, time to cut the cake."

"What about golf?"

"You better take a break so you don't wear yourself out, Willy. Eat some cake. There will be plenty of time for more golf. Besides, you haven't gotten to try out the putting green in the garage yet. JP and Emily spent a long time setting it up just for you."

Willy walked over and gave JP and Emily a big hug. "Thanks. You guys are the best."

Tears came to Emily's eyes and she gave Willy a kiss on the cheek and another big hug. When Willy returned to the cake, she turned to JP and said, "Isn't it amazing how Willy exemplifies what the Bible says, that we must become like children to enter the Kingdom of Heaven?"

"Amen to that," JP replied.

※ ※ ※

The armored vehicles parked about a half-block from Dr. Patrick's house and the two teams quickly headed to their positions. The security team surrounded the house on all sides and the entry team quietly approached the front door in single file. Captain Jameson trailed the entry team by a short distance, ready to give the command to go when his teams radioed they were in position. Sam had exited the armored vehicle and slowly made her way closer to the house, while staying in the street as she had been instructed.

The team leader on the security team radioed, "Security team in place."

This was quickly followed by "Ready at entry" from the entry team leader.

Captain Jameson activated his mike and said, "On my mark— one, two, go!"

The lead man at the door swung a hand-held battering ram that struck the front door of Dr. Patrick's house. The door shattered off its hinges and collapsed inward. The second man, who was posted out to the side, pointed his assault rifle at the door, as the third man tossed a flash grenade into the entryway, after making sure no one was just inside the door. A deafening explosion with a bright flash followed. The team then quickly entered.

Dr. Patrick's guests screamed as the door was knocked off its hinges. They saw a small canister thrown into the entryway and were stunned by the flash and the loud bang that followed. By the time the guests realized what had happened, the enforcement unit entry team was in the living room with their assault rifles pointed at them. The team members broke off in pairs and entered the various rooms, yelling "Clear" if they found no one inside.

JP and Emily were out in the garage putting with Willy on the putting green as the door to the garage flew open and two entry team members bolted through it. When the men entered, Emily looked up and reflexively raised the putter up in front of her. The lead man saw a glint off the putter, yelled "gun" and aimed his rifle at Emily. Willy jumped in front of her just as the officer fired his assault rifle.

Willy's putter flew from his hand and he fell to the ground. Blood quickly stained the front of his shirt, by his right shoulder.

"What are you doing?!" JP shouted as he started over toward Willy.

"Stay where you are," the officer screamed at JP.

"Not on your life," JP responded and continued over to Willy as Emily quickly bent down to put pressure on Willy's wound.

The officer keyed his two-way and said, "Medic, man down in the garage."

JP checked Willy and felt a strong pulse in his neck. JP took over for Emily and put pressure on the wound. Willy opened his eyes and said, "That hurts."

"Sorry Willy. You're going to be just fine. I just need to stop the bleeding."

"It's okay, JP."

The team medic entered the room and quickly came over. He looked at Willy and made a shocked observation: "He's a Down's."

JP replied, "He's a human being and he just saved my girlfriend from being shot. Do your job and treat him!"

"Okay. Just step back."

Through their radios, the team members then heard the word, "Centralize." They immediately motioned for JP and Emily to head back into the living room where the other guests were all corralled. As they entered the living room, Dr. Patrick turned to JP and said, "Where's Willy? Is he okay?"

"He's been shot. He's bleeding. The medic is checking him over right now."

Dr. Patrick started walking toward the garage door and the team leader shouted, "Stop!"

"I'm a surgeon and I'm going out to check on Willy."

The team leader reluctantly let him go, but sent another member of the team behind him with his rifle pointed at him. The team leader then spoke into his mike, "Ready for inspection, sir."

As Captain Jameson heard the words, he turned back toward Sam and said, "Do you want to go in?"

Sam replied, "Are you sure it's okay?"

"Not really, but you might be able to help identify some of the people. At least that's the reason I'll give officially. Besides, you probably won't get a chance like this again."

Sam walked up to the door and entered with the captain.

※ ※ ※

Lieutenant Osgood and his wife had been riding around town with the Minister of Health for about an hour and yet the minister had not said one word to them. Suddenly, the glass screen separating the front seats from the back slid down and the driver looked back at the minister in the rear view mirror. "They're in, sir," he said.

Dr. Atherton simply replied, "Take us there, please."

Jaye and Janet exchanged confused glances until Jaye finally said, "Sir, may I ask where we are going?"

Dr. Atherton looked over at them and said, "Redemption."

※ ※ ※

As the captain and Sam entered Dr. Patrick's house, the officers shouted, "Commander on deck!"

Sam quickly picked out JP and Emily and made eye contact. As she did, her face turned red and she looked down at the floor. She turned to Captain Jameson and whispered, "I'm sure Emily is the girl from the class."

Captain Jameson asked the team leader for a report and was led to the garage. As the captain entered the garage, he noticed an older individual caring for the victim, while the medic seemed to be taking orders. He gave the medic a dark look and turned to the older man. "May I ask who you are?"

"My name is Dr. Patrick. I'm a retired surgeon. May I ask just who you are and why you and your men have violently entered my home, frightened my guests, and shot one of them?"

"My name is Captain Jameson and we are from the Medical Enforcement Unit. We have reason to believe that at least two of your guests have committed crimes against the Medical Enforcement Act. Now that I see that the victim is a Down's man, you may be guilty of harboring an escaped person scheduled for termination. That too is punishable under the Medical Reconciliation Act."

※ ※ ※

The car the Osgoods were riding in came to a stop. Dr. Atherton opened the door. "Please follow me." The lieutenant and his wife stepped out of the vehicle into a quiet neighborhood. As they looked around, they saw that the street was lined with numerous other cars. The lieutenant looked down the street and recognized the MEU's armored vehicles. This confused him even further.

Minister Atherton began walking toward one of the houses, followed by the lieutenant and his wife. They entered the front entrance with the minister and words they had not heard for a long time quickly rang out.

"Mommy! Daddy!" Katie yelled as she ran over and jumped into the lieutenant's arms. Tears welled up in Janet and Jaye's eyes and they all three embraced for what seemed like an eternity.

The minister also was greeted unexpectedly by a familiar voice.

"Daddy?"

"Sam? What are you doing here?"

Sheepishly Sam replied, "I've been wanting to see what Mike did on his job so I talked him into letting me come along on a raid." She hoped her answer would prevent the captain from getting in trouble, but had little hope that it would.

"Just where is Captain Jameson?" asked the minister as he turned from Sam to the one of the officers standing guard in the living room.

"Sir, he is out in the garage. There was one man wounded as we conducted the raid."

"One of our men or one of these people?"

"One of them, sir."

The minister grimaced and proceeded out to the garage where he found the captain as well as the team medic and an older gentleman. They were attending to a man on the floor. "How is he?" he asked.

Dr. Patrick looked up and recognized Dr. Atherton. "He'll make it, no thanks to your men."

"I'm very sorry he was injured. I'm sure I'll get a full report."

"I need to get him treated."

"No doubt an ambulance is on its way."

"He can't go to the hospital."

Dr. Atherton walked over to take a closer look. "I understand. Is he stable enough to wait for a few minutes?"

"I believe he is. The medic has an IV running and I think the bullet passed through his shoulder without hitting a major artery."

"Good." The minister asked the medic to go out and get the lieutenant and his wife, as well as his own daughter who had accompanied the team on the raid.

When the medic approached them in the house, the lieutenant and his wife were reluctant to leave Katie, but Emily offered to watch her and Katie readily went to her. They followed the medic back to the garage and Sam reluctantly joined them. As they entered, the minister told the medic to return to the living room.

"But, sir, what about the wounded man?"

"I believe Dr. Patrick is more than capable of keeping tabs

on him."

"Yes, sir."

After the medic left, the garage was silent for a short time until the minister said, "It seems we have a situation here."

Captain Jameson quickly responded. "Sir we'll get these people into custody and get this wrapped up quickly. I think a good many of these people are either involved with the Underground or are fugitives from the End of Life Care Center."

"I'm sorry, Mike, but that's not quite the situation I was talking about."

"If you mean there's a problem because of Sam coming along, I take full respons—"

"No, no, Captain. That's not what I'm talking about either. The problem is, I can't let you arrest any of these people."

"I don't quite follow you, sir," the captain replied with a puzzled look on his face.

"You see, Mike, these people all work for me. I'm the regional leader of the Underground."

"Daddy, you can't be serious."

"Oh, I'm very serious, Sam. I've been opposed to the Medical Reconciliation Act from day one. I just decided to fight it from the inside rather than the outside."

The captain hesitated, but then he unholstered his gun. "In that case, sir, I have no choice but to arrest you also."

"Mike!" Sam exclaimed. "You can't be serious."

"I have no choice, Sam."

"Put that away, Captain. You do have another choice, but you may not like it."

"Sir?"

"You're going to bring this raid to a conclusion, make no arrests, and leave with your men."

"Why would I do that, sir? This is probably the biggest bust since the institution of the Act."

"I'm not finished. You're also going to resign in the next couple of days and Lieutenant Osgood will be replacing you as head of the enforcement unit."

The captain chuckled incredulously. "Why would I want to just walk away from this and then resign?"

"It seems, Captain, that unless you comply with my wishes, you will come down with a terminal illness that will land you in the End of Life Care Center."

"What are you talking about, Daddy? Mike's as healthy as a horse."

"I know that and, at the present time, everyone else knows that. Unfortunately, if he does not do what I say, the Ministry file on him will show that he indeed does have a terminal illness and he will be scheduled for termination. I've made certain arrangements that would go into effect whether I were incarcerated or not."

"That's blackmail!"

"I'm quite aware of what it is, Captain, and I truly had hoped it would never have to come to this. Unfortunately, this situation appears to have no other solution."

"Daddy, you wouldn't really terminate the man I love, would you?"

"I didn't know your relationship had gone that far, but I have no choice. He, on the other hand, does have a choice. Through my connections, I have already arranged a new position for him with the police department in New York City. It may not be what he had planned for his life, but it's a good opportunity and has great potential for advancement, especially with his background. I'd say it's a pretty good choice compared to the alternative."

The lieutenant and his wife looked at each other with disbelief on their faces as they watched the captain almost stumble back into a chair.

He sat silently for a moment and then Sam went over to him. "I'm so sorry Mike. I had no idea about any of this. You know, I do love you and I don't want anything to happen to you. I think we could be happy in New York."

"What do you mean 'we?' What about med school?"

"I don't really think my heart has ever been in it. I would really love to pursue my music and New York would be a great place to do that."

"It seems I don't really have any other choice."

Dr. Atherton walked over to the captain. "I'm not really happy about Sam quitting school and going to New York with you, but she is a grown woman and she has to make her own decisions. So what do you say?"

Captain Jameson stood up and looked at Dr. Atherton face to face for about a minute then held out his hand. "I don't agree with what you're doing, sir, but I do appreciate the fact that you follow your convictions and that you are least giving me an option."

Dr. Atherton shook his hand. "Is it a deal?"

"It's a deal."

Sam walked over and gave her father and Captain Jameson hugs.

"Sam, are you sure you want to give up med school for music?"

"You know music has always been my first love. I'm sure and besides, where Mike goes, I go. That is, if that's what he wants."

"You know I do, Sam."

"Okay, then. Captain, if you'll be so kind as to get your men to withdraw, I have some more unfinished business here. Would you also see to it that Sam gets home?"

"Yes, sir," said Captain Jameson as he put his arm out for Sam and headed out of the garage.

"Well, Lieutenant, or should I now say, Captain? Are you up

to this?"

"Yes, sir, but what are the men going to say? After all, I was caught dealing with the Underground."

"You were on special assignment for me to try and ferret out more members of the Underground. We had to arrest you to make it look plausible, in case we needed you to do some more undercover work. I think they'll buy it, especially coming from the Minister of Health. Obviously, we now know secrets about each other that could get us in deep trouble. We'll just have to call it a draw and trust each other."

"No problem there, sir. What about Katie?"

"Unfortunately, there is nothing I can do about that. She is already in the system as having been scheduled for termination. The Underground can continue to treat her and, if she is cured, the best option for her will be to change her name. If anyone aware of her status saw her with you, she could be picked up again. We can arrange a new home and identity for her. When she's a little older, all can be explained to her, and hopefully, you can reunite."

The lieutenant looked at his wife who slowly shook her head indicating they really had no choice. "Okay, sir, but we would like a little time to talk to her to see if we can help her understand."

"You go ahead. I'll be out in a little bit. I just need to talk to Dr. Patrick for a few minutes."

The lieutenant and Janet left the garage and went in to talk to Katie. Dr. Atherton finally turned to Dr. Patrick. "I've looked forward to meeting you for a long time. It's too bad it had to be like this. Hopefully this young man will be okay."

"I'm pretty sure he'll be just fine. I take it you can handle the medic, since he's aware that Willy has Down's syndrome?"

"That shouldn't be a problem. We'll just tell him he was taken to the termination center. He'll have no way to verify that."

"Good. Willy's been with us for a long time."

"I'd better get the Osgoods home. Again, it is a pleasure getting to meet you. Keep up the good work, and be careful."

The minister left the garage and Dr. Patrick knelt back down to check Willy. "How's it going, good buddy?"

"I'm okay, Dr. John. Can we go home now?"

"You bet. I need to patch you up anyway."

Dr. Patrick went out to the living room to get JP and a couple of the other men to help him with Willy. All of Captain Jameson's men had already left and Dr. Atherton was just leaving with the Osgoods. Katie was with Emily and it was obvious she had been crying.

JP was perplexed. "Grandpa, what's going on? Wasn't that the Minister of Health?"

"Yes. it was. As I said before, the less you know, the better. Suffice it to say everything is okay for now. I need your help with Willy."

JP and a couple of the other guests helped Willy to Father Mark's car. JP, Emily, and Katie rode back to the church with Willy and Dr. Patrick followed in his own vehicle. The remainder of the guests departed at the same time and the long-awaited party came to a premature end.

Epilogue

Sam and Captain Jameson had moved to New York shortly after he had resigned from the Medical Enforcement Unit and she had withdrawn from medical school. Through Dr. Atherton's connections, Jameson had secured a position as detective in the city's police department. He had already advanced up to a lieutenant rank and was thoroughly enjoying his new job.

※ ※ ※

Sam had begun the arduous task of reacquainting herself with the world of music. She enrolled in singing lessons, auditioned for roles in various Broadway productions, and up until now had been unsuccessful. However, her persistence and hard work had finally paid off. She had landed a small but substantial role in her first show. Although it was not the lead, she had two solos as well as a few speaking lines.

Dr. Atherton, of course, had a front-row seat and Lieutenant Jameson sat next to him. Despite their past differences they had developed at least a friendly relationship. They chatted until the lights dimmed. The curtain went up and both smiled as Sam walked on to the stage.

※ ※ ※

Graduation from medical school was a huge affair. Family members came from all over to see their loved ones finally become doctors. The event was taking place in a much larger auditorium than the one JP had been in over two years ago when he had first heard the Kevorkian Oath recited. It seemed like a long time ago. So much had happened since then and his life was on a different course.

He and Emily had been married for about nine months and she was five months pregnant. The thought of being married and soon becoming a father was a little overwhelming at times, but he couldn't have been happier. They had also unofficially adopted Katie and she too was excited about having a new brother or sister.

JP had decided to do a surgery residency and was looking forward to getting started. His grandfather had played a role in that decision. JP hoped he could become the surgeon that his grandfather had been, and still was for that matter.

The Underground remained active. They'd had had their ups and downs, but continued on with their mission. Willy had recovered from the gunshot wound and was back at the safe house, helping with all who passed through there.

As JP paraded in with the other graduates, he looked over and caught a glimpse of his grandfather and Emily. Both were beaming with pride as they watched him walk by them. His father was present also, but looked much more subdued.

One by one, the various speakers droned on about the responsibilities the students would soon have and some continued to stress the importance of how the good of all outweighed the good of the individual. JP thought back to all those he had come to know and help by his work in the Underground.

Once the graduation ceremony ended, the students were all asked to stand for the recitation of the Kevorkian Oath. JP stood with the rest, but as the others were reciting that oath, he recited the Hippocratic Oath to himself from memory. He recalled the first time he had read it, standing in his grandfather's living room. While he recited it, he turned and looked at his grandfather. They smiled at each other as their lips moved in unison.

CPSIA information can be obtained at www.ICGtesting.com
Printed in the USA
BVOW04s1751110315

391222BV00002B/516/P

9 781633 930889